EMM

Curse of the Dearmad

of the

ILLUSTRATED BY

HANNAH JESSE

TINY TREE
CHILDREN'S BOOKS

First Published 2021
Tiny Tree Children's Books
(an imprint of Matthew James Publishing Ltd)
Unit 46, Goyt Mill
Marple
Stockport
SK6 7HX

www.tinytreebooks.com

ISBN: 978-1-913230-19-7

Illustrations ©Hannah Jesse

For Orry and Judy, I wrote this for you

For Ian, I wrote this because of you

ACKNOWLEDGEMENTS

I'd like to thank James and Ant at Tiny Tree for being the most supportive and hard-working team ever. Thank you for giving opportunities to new voices, and for picking my book. I will always be thankful that I took a punt and sent it your way.

Huge thanks to Emma Roberts, the kindest and most thoughtful editor I could ever have hoped to work with. Thank you for treading softly, and for teaching me so much.

Thank you Adam Creed, AKA Gareth Creer, AKA dad. Your notes and encouragement, and the example you set, are the reasons I kept writing when life was trying to get in the way.

To Fiona Gell, thank you for being so generous with your time and for sharing your awe inspiring sea-based expertise. If it weren't for you, the eels might still be doing the conga.

Much love to the Good Ship for all the cheerleading and support. You really are a wonderful bunch.

Finally, Ian. Thank you for giving me the greatest gift a writer could ask for: time. There aren't enough words to express how much your support means to me. Thank you for showing me Cornaa and for giving me our two little miracles. Without these things, Curse of the Dearmad would never have come to be.

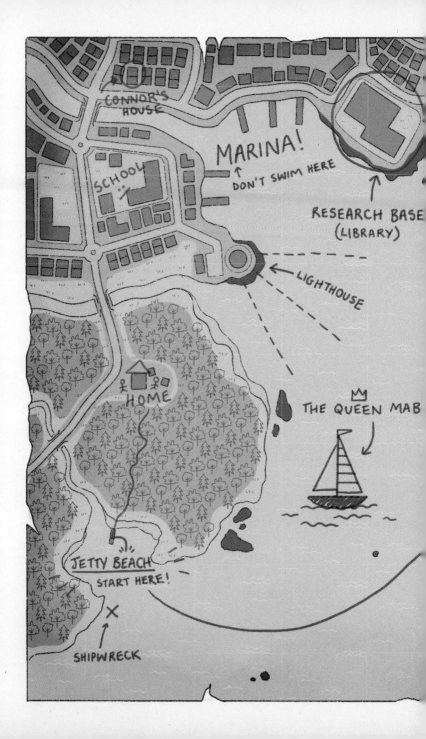

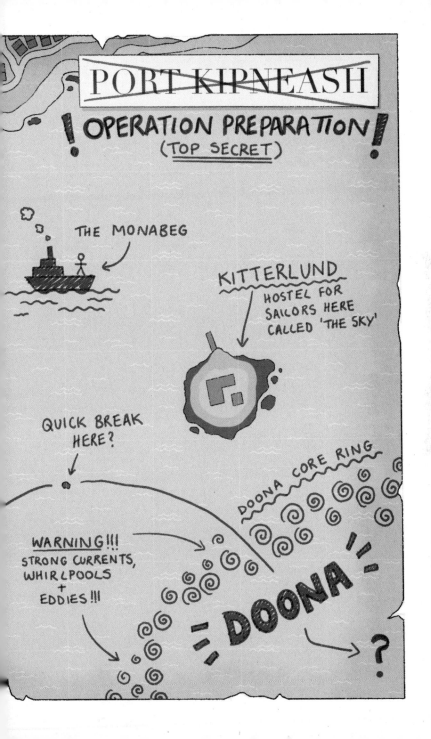

gilly

(gi-li)

noun

A person with paired respiratory organs (known also as 'gills') by which oxygen is extracted from water and can be inherited from the mother, father or both parents. Gills are located on the neck and are usually pink in colour, circular and no bigger than a five pence coin. Gills enable a gilly to exist under water for long periods of time. Other common features include webbed feet and an urgent need to spend time in the sea in order to establish and maintain good health.

Example in use:

'that gilly child looks unwell, perhaps he has not been to the sea lately'.

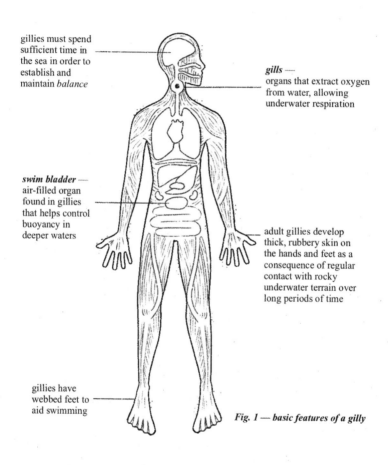

gillies must spend sufficient time in the sea in order to establish and maintain *balance*

gills —
organs that extract oxygen from water, allowing underwater respiration

swim bladder —
air-filled organ found in gillies that helps control buoyancy in deeper waters

adult gillies develop thick, rubbery skin on the hands and feet as a consequence of regular contact with rocky underwater terrain over long periods of time

gillies have webbed feet to aid swimming

Fig. 1 — basic features of a gilly

Chapter 1

The Secret Resourcefulness of Connor Price

CONNOR

Connor Price was hatching an audacious plan. And this time he would follow it through. No fear. There was nothing left to lose.

The hour was late and the house was still. Connor had not been to sleep at all. He reached over to his bedside table, almost knocking over a tall glass of green juice, untouched since his mum had placed it there this morning. Full of vitamins, none of which would do any damn good. He flicked a switch and his lamp came on. With the shock of light to his fragile senses, he rubbed his eyes and sat up in his bed.

He ran a finger along the bare flesh of his arm, mapping the green and purple veins which carried his tired blood around his exhausted body. His skin, like a pathetic veil of translucent cloth, was colourless and paper thin. It felt like his organs were on display for all to see. He locked his eyelids tightly together. Splashes of neon and echoes of colour pulsed in his brain; they were the imprints left behind by light. Quickly his eyes adjusted to the black. In the stillness of his room he summoned the memory of cold salt water rushing through his gills, making him strong.

The sea was calling Connor, but Janie Price would never change her mind. It was an abyss filled with danger and probable death. She had seen it before; she would not let the sea take her son too. Deep sea swimming was strictly rationed, saved only for when Connor's father returned from his work on board the *Monabeg*.

There had been visits to the shore, of course. Paddling hand in hand with his mum, wading through the shallows of the estuary, but only if she agreed that he was strong enough. There had even been a swim last week, his first in over a month. But Connor was in no rush to do *that* again.

'Connor?' Janie had called to him as he swam away from the shore, towards the buoy. 'Connor!' she'd screamed. 'Connor! Connor!' she'd wailed at the sea.

'I'm OK,' he had called back, feebly. He'd been tempted to keep swimming, to dive under and not come back until he'd had his fill.

'It's too much! Come back, you're too weak! Connor!' she'd cried, pacing the shore and throwing her arms about, summoning him back to her. Everyone on the beach had turned to look, people had started to gather. Connor swam back, eyes full of tears, heart full of a heavy, wordless rage.

Janie's fears were confirmed. Connor took ill later that night. But the illness was a symptom of the burden on his soul, not the pressure on his body.

And so, in his bed in the wee small hours of the last seven days, Connor Price had been hatching a plan. Each night since that disastrous day at the beach, Connor had been plotting what he must do to take matters into his own hands. Decisively and finally. And tonight was the night. There was no wimping out. This was life or death.

Connor flicked the light-switch again and his room fell back into darkness. He listened carefully as Janie turned off the TV, closed windows and locked doors. The cats were out on their night-time rampages, and the washing up was all done. He heard her walk up the stairs, her delicate feet tiptoeing up the creaky steps, trying not to wake him. He heard her brush her teeth and yawn. She gave a little chuckle; he wondered what at.

Her phone rang.

'Hello?' she whispered. 'Oh, Jonah, hello darling... yes he's fine, fast asleep, dead to the world.' The house was silent but for his mother's soft tones. 'Oh, yes, we can't wait to see you... we miss you... Yes, you too, stay safe, I do worry about... I love you too, see you tomorrow then, night-night,' and she hung up.

His door opened with a creak and he could sense his mother's presence in the room. She brushed the hair from his face with her soft fingertips and kissed his forehead gently. He needed a cut but had been too poorly to go to the hairdressers. He refused to let Janie do it herself any more. Previous results had not been good.

She pulled the covers up around him, tucking him in tightly. He stayed as still as a rock set in the watery deep, resisting the urge to grab hold of her, to cling to her warmth, to remain in her protective arms forever. He felt ashamed of his plotting, it felt like a betrayal.

She walked away.

Connor listened as she closed his door, and then a few seconds later, her own door. He waited for the *thump*. Every night there was one. Twelve minutes passed before the *thump* came tonight. He pictured her trying to keep her eyes open, trying to fight her tiredness, but eventually losing the battle and dropping her heavy book on to the floor as she fell asleep mid-sentence.

He gave it another ten minutes. Just to be safe.

Connor Price could hear his own bones creak. He was sure he could. He sometimes worried that his skin might flake off or tear like tissue under the weight of his clothes. He gently pulled on his swimming trunks, a hooded sweater and his socks. Downstairs, he squeezed his feet into his trainers, barely worn, still bright white, but starting to feel tight.

Had Janie known what Connor was up to, she would have worried about the cold more than anything else. But Connor knew he would not feel it in the water. He was built for the water.

He snuck out into the dark of the night, across Port Kipneash, towards the edge of the sea.

Four months felt like four years to Connor, but Kipneash was still so new to him, so different to the Indian Ocean, so much the worse with Jonah away for weeks on end.

Connor walked quickly through the town, not strong enough to run. He passed the cottages and rickety shops that lined the main promenade. The sky was clear and still, and the moon was full. He pulled down his hood a little lower as he dragged his tired bones on, limping past The Tangled Web pub where the croaky old fishermen drank their ale.

Finally, he reached the marina, the final frontier of his carefully laid plan. There was no one around but still he felt eyes on him. He didn't care. He snuck on to the harbour jetty through the maze of fishing boats, sail-boats, tugs and yachts. He scurried to the end of the jetty and hid his shoes, socks and sweater behind an abandoned pile of thick, sea-worn rope. Out of breath, he strapped on his head torch and didn't even stop to see if anyone was looking. He jumped in.

No one had told him not to swim in the mucky waters of the harbour, but tonight he learned that lesson. He was squeamish about the feel of the algae on the ropes of the boats, and the slithery seaweed around the harbour. He didn't like the look of the dogfish that circled brutishly, looking for scraps. There was a faint taste of petrol coming through his gills. None of this was good.

He felt no better. For several days afterwards he would feel much worse. But he knew now that he could do it on his own, and that was all that mattered. The conger eels had not scared him off with their gummy, satisfied smirks, and their eyes as black as night. They loitered around the boats, around his feet, his arms, but they were no threat.

And no one had caught him. No one had stopped him and put him back in bed to slowly wither, the victim of a life half-lived.

From that night on, he would not return to the harbour. Emboldened by his first night-time mission, he studied his father's map of the town and decided upon a more ambitious route down through the wood on the edge of Port Kipneash, to the long grass and the sandy banks of the estuary. The estuary was his gateway, where the sea glistened under the stars, by the glow of the lighthouse. It welcomed him in.

The sea would make him better. He truly believed it would.

At last Connor Price had this to be proud of: he was saving his own life.

He was soon a professional at night swimming. His skin began to turn a healthy pink, his gills were no longer crusted and sore. Within a few months he was well enough for his mother to agree to school.

And she never knew.

No one ever did.

Chapter 2

*The Fateful Meeting of Connor Price
and Percy Shearwater*

PERCY

'Are you nervous, Percy?' asked Nell as they turned the corner.

'Why would I be?' Percy said, kicking a stone as he walked. It rarely occurred to Percy to be nervous.

'I don't know. It's a bit weird though, don't you think?'

Percy looked at his twin. She wasn't easily rattled, but he could tell she was worried about today. She kept tucking loose strands of hair behind her ear and had been unusually quiet since they'd left for school. Percy didn't know how to reassure his sister, or even if he really wanted to. He considered mocking her new, highly polished, crease-free school shoes and the brand new rucksack that sat primly on her straight-as-an-arrow back. But he couldn't be bothered with it; she'd most likely have a strong comeback that would put him in his place anyway.

'It's not really that weird. We used to go to *that* school,' Percy pointed to the other side of the road where Port Kipneash Primary stood with its brightly coloured rainbow fence and playground full of monkey bars and mums with prams. 'And now we go to *this* school.' He nodded, eyes fixed on Bellsalla, the only high school in Port Kipneash. No coloured fence. No mums with prams. No climbing frames.

'Hmm,' murmured Nell. 'I suppose.'

'Are *you* nervous?' asked Percy.

'Not really,' she paused, chewing on her fingernail then reaching up high to ruffle her brother's hair. It was longer and shaggier than usual, and had been bleached by the long summer days out at sea and on the beach. Percy hadn't been anywhere near a hairbrush in weeks. Usually their mam was strict on those kinds of things, but she'd been somewhat distracted lately.

'Get off.' Percy pushed Nell away and charged towards a huddle of boys who were crowded around Bobby McGiven, as usual. Percy hadn't seen any of them all summer and he wondered briefly if they might have noticed. But, as always, the boys smiled to see Percy, their effervescent friend, and greeted him with the usual slaps on the back and punching of arms. No one seemed irked by his summer-long absence. Everyone knew he was different and they just accepted it. Being a gilly didn't make Percy Shearwater a bad friend, it just explained why he wasn't always there for afternoons hanging around on bikes at the harbour, or bus trips to the bowling alley and the arcade in the city.

Nell walked up and stood silently behind her brother, inspecting the surroundings for familiar faces.

'Did you have a good summer, Bobby?' asked Percy.

'I was just telling the lads, I went to London. It was so good. I saw Belgium from the top of the London Eye, honestly,' boasted Bobby with a grin.

'Well, *that's* a lie,' hissed Nell under her breath, just loud enough for Bobby to hear – if he was listening, which he wasn't. Bobby never listened.

'Most days me and my cousins just rode the Tube, took our skateboards to the Southbank, went to Camden Market, it was pretty cool.' Bobby's big mane of golden curls was shaking and bouncing as he talked. 'You know what *the Tube* is, right? *The Underground?* It was pretty awesome. I'm going to live in London when I'm done with this place.'

Percy was genuinely impressed and intrigued. Nell was less so.

'Percy,' Nell growled at him in a sharp whisper as the children dispersed and made their way to the now-open doors of Bellsalla.

'What?'

'Erm... *Yes Bobby, you are AMAZING Bobby, that sounds totally AMAZING,*' she mocked. 'There is absolutely zero chance that Bobby's mum would let him go on the Tube on his own. *Zero.* It's just bizarre that he'd even try to get away with a lie like that.' She shook her head.

Percy gave his sister a half-laugh.

'Don't laugh, Percy. It's annoying. *He's* annoying. He's such a liar. Percy... *Percy?* Are you even listening to me?'

Percy shrugged and carried on walking.

'Do you want to know what's amazing? Spending the summer swimming with a leatherback turtle and hanging out with dolphins. *That's* awesome. I bet most of those boys don't even stop to think why you've not been around all summer.'

21

The summer coming to an end was bitter-sweet. Nell was right. But Percy liked to focus more on the sweet than the bitter.

'Anyway, it's good we've got Mrs Angkor. She's great, don't you think?' said Nell, eyes wide and glistening.

'Yeah, I guess,' smiled Percy as he nodded and waved to the friends he spied through gaps in the throng as they filed down the corridor. Familiar faces were not unchanged by the long summer break; being in high school made everyone look a little different. Maybe Nell was right to find it a bit weird after all.

The children funnelled into Class 7A, navigating the politics of where to sit and who to avoid. Percy hung back to see where his friends were. Politics did not bother Nell; Percy smiled to himself and shook his head at the predictability of his sister as she rushed towards the table that was both nearest the front and nearest the window. A prime position to maximize learning.

Mrs Angkor began counting back from five, growing more irritated with every number until she reached one, by which time all of the children were sitting, at their tables, finishing conversations with whispers that they hoped would be unheard, or ignored.

Although petite, Mrs Angkor was formidable. She wore thick-rimmed, round glasses and always had a black skirt and black jumper on. It was odd, because all of the children knew her from the bakery that her husband owned in Port Kipneash. When they saw her there on Saturdays she wore the most brightly coloured clothes, and she didn't have her glasses on.

'I can still hear you *speaking...*' spat Mrs Angkor angrily, and the speaking stopped.

A knock on the door broke the silence.

'Come in!' barked Mrs Angkor. The door slowly creaked open and a pair of blue eyes peered around it. 'Ah, you must be Connor, come in, have you completed enrolment?'

A small boy walked into the room, pale as a sheet with hair as black as night.

'Yes,' he whispered.

'Connor is new to Port Kipneash,' Mrs Angkor told the class. 'Most of you will know at least a few others in our class from Port Kipneash Primary or perhaps further afield on the island, but Connor won't know anyone at all, so I hope that you will all make him feel very welcome.'

Connor faced the rest of the children in 7A and gave a small embarrassed wave with his right hand, as he lowered his chin and self-consciously raised his left hand to his neck. It was in this tiniest of gestures that Percy realised what was happening. Connor was attempting to conceal something that was plainly obvious to Percy, if not to everyone in the room. Connor's gills were bright red, a beacon demanding attention. They were sore and shone with an unhealthy sheen of mucus that Percy had rarely experienced himself. Percy may have spotted it first, but everyone could surely see that the boy stood at the front of the room was a gilly.

Not even Percy Shearwater was immune to that special kind of lonely that comes from being different to everyone else, and so the sight of another gilly boy filled him with feeling that, had he been asked, he would not have been able to explain. He was hit by a rushing wave. The feeling pulsed through his veins, rushed through his gills. His breath rose sharply in his chest and the whole class turned to look at him with the sound of it. His chair made a loud scraping noise as he rose to his feet. Suddenly, no one was looking at Connor any more and all the attention in the room was on Percy. Percy stared at Connor's neck with his eyes wide, and growing wider, and his mouth agape.

'Would you like to sit with our new classmate, Percy?' said Mrs Angkor.

Percy realised that everyone was looking at him. But he was not embarrassed. Percy rarely felt embarrassed. He was used to people staring at him.

As he walked slowly towards Connor, the rest of the class stared at Percy's seldom-seen serious face. Percy glanced at his teacher for reassurance before he took the empty seat next to his fellow gilly. She smiled and gave a nod, then cleared her throat and began the register, fiddling with the glasses she did not need to wear.

When Mrs Angkor came to Nell's name in the register there was no sound, no response. Percy looked over to Nell, every teacher's best student, never slow to answer any question, and especially not her own name. Nell wiped her cheek dry with the sleeve of her school cardigan. She wore a smile that mirrored the one beaming across Connor Price's face.

There was no way that Percy could have known it then, in that classroom, in front of his friends and teacher, but a time would come when warm smiles between his sister and his friend would be as lost as a forgotten memory. Lost in the cold swell of the faraway sea.

Chapter 3

The Three Embarrassments of Connor Price

CONNOR

'Will you tell Mam I'm at Connor's? I'll be home at six,' Percy said to Nell as they left the gates.

Nell gave a nod and turned her back. She walked away with two other girls who were both laughing. Connor didn't know if maybe he should be asking Nell to come for tea too, seeing as she and Percy were twins. But she was gone before he could ask.

'What do you think they're laughing at?' he asked Percy.

'Dunno. Probably something stupid.' Percy grinned.

Connor nodded.

'So you've *never* been to school before?' asked Percy as they walked away from Bellsalla.

'Not for a long time, no. I've been pretty sick most of my life. One of my gills...' Connor hesitated, his hand moving instinctively towards his neck to stroke the delicate skin around his left gill. 'I've got a weakness, and I guess I've never really found balance.'

Percy nodded like he understood, but Connor wasn't sure that he did.

Connor could barely believe that Percy was the real deal; it had taken him all morning to convince himself that Percy might be a true gilly.

At break-time Connor had said to Percy, *let me see your gills properly, they're hardly even there.* Percy revealed the small pink circles on each side of his neck just below his ears, almost hidden by his long unkempt hair and his school shirt.

'Yours look a bit red – mine get like that when I've got a cold.' Percy smiled.

Connor was embarrassed.

What would Percy have said if he'd seen Connor's gills three months ago, back when they were crusted and weeping like open sores? Connor had even been known to have gills that bled, they were so delicate. At one point they became so scaly that he was worried people might think he was turning into a fish. His left gill was too small; it'd always been that way, he sometimes felt like that's what stopped him from being a strong gilly. A real gilly. A gilly like Percy Shearwater.

Percy looked so healthy, with his broad swimmer's back and his wide grin. He was so tall, Connor felt tiny next to him. His skin had the ruddy glow of good health. Connor felt a pang of jealousy. Percy was strong; Percy had found balance.

Connor had delicate features, a small pointy nose and bright red lips. He was small for his age and carried no meat on his bones, though he had become more muscular of late, and his cheeks had taken on a pinkish hue.

'This is my house,' said Connor as they walked towards his door.

Connor turned the key in the lock. Janie had been burning one of her candles and the house smelled sweet and clean.

'Connor, is that you?' her voice called from the kitchen. 'I wish you would've let me meet you at the gate...' She appeared from the kitchen, flinging a tea towel over her shoulder. She stopped when she saw Percy. 'Hello.' She smiled. 'So, who do we have here?'

Janie was beaming and Connor knew why. He'd only had a couple of friends back in Limiona. Janie always worried that he didn't make friends easily.

'This is Percy, Percy Shearwater.'

She nodded, like she knew the name.

'Hello, Percy. You're stopping for tea?'

'Yes please, Mrs Price.'

The boys went upstairs. Connor didn't know what to say, he was silent while Percy looked at the posters on his walls, the books on his shelf, the figures and trinkets dotted around his almost-tidy room. It felt strange, another boy being in his room, making himself at home in the space that had been Connor's prison all summer long. Except for the night-time, when he was free. As the boys lay on the floor playing on Connor's Xbox, Percy filled Connor in on who was who in Class 7A and every embarrassing incident that had ever happened to every child in the class when they were all still at primary school.

'Tommy Kerruish is the worst.' Percy laughed loudly. 'He thinks he's tough but he called Mr Jones *mummy* on a regular basis when we were in Class Three.'

'Seriously?'

'Seriously! It was a regular thing, no joke! It was by accident of course, but every time he did it the whole class would go nuts, and he'd be so ashamed he'd start throwing pencils around the room and stuff.'

'Who? The teacher?'

'No! Of course not.' This tickled Percy and he rolled on the floor in tucks of laughter. 'Tommy!'

Connor laughed too.

'Can you imagine Mr Jones, throwing pencils about though? That'd be hilarious.' Percy sighed, his raucous laughter simmering to a breathless giggle. 'There's no hiding from mistakes in Port Kipneash, even if you were seven when you made them.'

The boys settled, still and quiet, thumbs twiddling, all eyes on FIFA.

'Boys!' Janie's voice rose up the stairs with the delicious, fatty smell of chips and the whirring sound of the oven fan.

The boys sat at the table. Connor could tell something was bothering Percy. His eyebrows were fixed in a concerned frown, his gaze drawing towards the clock on the wall then blinking away as Janie tried to ask them about school.

'I suppose you're used to all this school stuff. But it must be exciting even for you, Percy, starting at the high school?' asked Janie.

'Not really... well, maybe, I haven't really thought about it to be honest. Today was a bit different. I've never met a gilly boy like me at school before, so that's something,' replied Percy kindly, before glancing at the clock again.

'It's funny that there aren't many gilly children in Port Kipneash, I really thought there'd be more.' Janie smiled.

'Gillies tend to move to the Indian Ocean when they have kids, that's what my mam says. But she won't move. Not ever,' explained Percy.

'That's where we're from.' Connor nodded in agreement. 'Limiona.'

Percy's knee was bouncing up and down with a nervousness that surprised Connor. 'Are you OK?' he asked as he watched Percy scoff down the last piece of pizza in a hurry. Janie disappeared from the room, their plates in her hands.

'When are we going?' said Percy, wriggling, shifty.

'What do you mean?'

'The sun's going to go soon, we could do with getting out, couldn't we? Will your mam come too?' asked Percy innocently.

It dawned on Connor that Percy was ready to go to the sea.

'Oh, no... I don't go swimming every day,' said Connor, embarrassed for the second time that day. 'My mum doesn't like it.'

There was a long silence. Percy looked shocked. Connor looked over his shoulder into the kitchen to check that his mum couldn't hear. 'My mum's a bit clueless when it comes to gillies. *Very* clueless, actually. Pretty weird seeing as she married one and gave birth to one.' Connor chuckled nervously. 'She's scared of the sea, doesn't like me going out on my own and, well, it's hard for us to swim out that much together. We don't go far.'

'Oh. So your dad's the gilly then? He's not... he's not *dead*, is he?'

'No!' Connor laughed again, this time with less nerves. 'No, he works on the *Monabeg*.'

Percy gave a nod. The *Monabeg* was the gilly research ship that circled the island and monitored the sea and the condition of the marine wildlife; there couldn't be many gillies alive who had not heard of it. Connor's father, Jonah, always said it was only gillies who worked on the *Monabeg* because it was only gillies who cared about the ocean these days. *They'd care about the sea too if their lives depended on it like ours do,* Jonah would say. These conversations left Connor feeling fearful and he hoped that his father wasn't right.

'Things are pretty tough on the *Monabeg* right now,' Connor went on, 'what with all the pollution and the diseased fish and everything. My dad is a specialist in marine wildlife, preserving it, looking after it. He says his job's getting harder, which makes sense.'

Percy nodded again. 'It worries my mam, *that's* for sure.'

'He's pretty senior, so he has to go away a lot... I mean *loads*. It was even worse when we lived in Limiona – he was away all the time then. He worked on the *Cousteau*.'

Connor felt good boasting about his father. The *Cousteau* research ship was even more famous than the *Monabeg*, and it was based in Limiona. It was the world's most highly regarded oceanic research vessel and it was founded and crewed entirely by gillies. The scientists who worked on the *Cousteau* were talented beyond compare: it was generally accepted that no one in the world knew the world's oceans like they did. Several members of the crew had been involved in the construction of a polar research vessel which garnered worldwide praise for its importance and ground-breaking scientific capabilities. Jonah Price was one of that crew.

The warmer seas, together with the fact that it was where the *Cousteau* was based, were the two reasons most gillies lived in Limiona, in the Indian Ocean. Connor was so proud of his dad, but missing him created such pain, he couldn't even begin to explain how it felt.

Percy was quiet. In a low whisper, he said, 'I don't know what I'd do if I didn't swim every day. Or even every week. I think I'd probably *die*.'

At that moment, and with an exceptionally unfortunate stroke of bad luck, Janie Price walked in with milkshakes and brownies on a tray. Percy did not see the look of pure horror on her face; his back was to the door. But Connor saw it, and a burning knot rose in his chest as the tray slipped idly from his mother's grip.

There was a huge crash. Connor knew Percy had not planned for Janie to hear, but he really wished his new friend had kept that particular thought to himself. Connor looked down, it was hard seeing his mum crying. He felt embarrassed for a third time.

'It's OK! It's OK! Nothing's smashed!' said Janie as she rubbed her damp cheek with the cuff of her cardigan and knelt to the floor, mopping up the milk with a tea-towel. Without looking his mother in the eye, knowing that he would find it impossible not to cry if he did, Connor got down on the floor to help her. Percy picked up a glass that had rolled to the other side of the room.

It was time for Percy to go home. They bundled into the car and made their way to the Shearwaters' cottage on the edge of Port Kipneash. It was only a short drive, but the gentle motion of the car was rocking Connor to sleep. He slow-blinked, desperately trying to keep his leaden eyelids open while his mother and friend chatted quietly in the front of the car about Mrs Angkor, and homework, and all the *normal* things that were now part of his life. But tiredness gripped him.

Tumbling in and out of sleep, Connor witnessed one last exchange that turned this special day from a wonderful one to a momentous one, and undid all of the minor trauma of his three embarrassments.

Connor heard his mother say to Percy, with a tremble in her voice that he would never forget, 'I know Connor would love to go out swimming with you, and your mum, or if you go alone... I mean... if your mum and dad let you go on your own... if they think that's safe... maybe you could go out together, maybe make it a regular thing?'

'I'd really like that, Mrs Price,' said Percy. 'And don't worry, I'll ask my mum to come too. Connor will be OK.'

They were at Percy's house. He got out of the car and said thank you for dinner.

Connor was too tired to open his eyes; he whispered, 'thank you Percy,' and Percy walked away.

With that, Connor knew he had found a good friend, and that his mum would be happy. Percy would never let him down, would never abandon him, come what may.

That night Connor slept the deepest, most peaceful, dreamless sleep that he had ever slept before.

But even the best of friends have weaknesses. Even the truest of people can falter.

Chapter 4

Just Another Swim

PERCY

'Can we go? I feel like my skin is itching,' said Percy with a shiver.

'One day off will do you no harm at all,' replied Mam.

'Please. Just ten minutes?'

'Percy, it's never just ten minutes.'

'Can I go on my own?'

'Not in the dark!' shouted Goldie from the living room.

Percy's dad didn't understand the urgency of his son's

immediate need to go swimming. He didn't understand that, after his first long day back at school, and everything that had happened that day, Percy needed it now more than ever. Goldie wasn't a gilly.

'Fine. Fine, ten minutes,' said Dina. She looked tired, her skin was grey. Percy was so hell-bent on going out that he either did not see it, or chose to ignore it. But Dina looked weak.

Goldie wandered over, he seemed uneasy, edgy. 'I'm not sure, Di—'

Dina cut him short. 'It's OK.'

Percy was desperate to swim. He couldn't stop thinking about Connor's gills, and how they were like the red-raw winter nostrils of a toddler.

The Shearwaters' rose-covered cottage was hidden in the middle of a forest at the edge of Port Kipneash. It was small and creaky, with stone and wooden floors and a stove downstairs that heated the whole house. The family drew lots for going to the coal bunker; Nell hated it the most, especially in the rain. Despite the rattling and clanging of the heat-conducting pipes, the warmth from their monstrous fire never really made its way upstairs to their beds, which were sometimes so cold they felt damp.

Downstairs was one big space. Two rooms punctuated only by two small steps that separated the family room from the kitchen. The ceiling was low, which made long-limbed Goldie look like even more of a gangly giant. He complained endlessly about banging his head, but never suggested they move.

'Don't be long,' warned Goldie as Percy slammed the door behind him, overtaking Dina as they made their way to Jetty Beach, dusk descending.

The dark and wild pine forest morphed into a glen that was flooded with living green and light that shone, mottled and tenacious, through the trees. A rocky stream led down to the sea, ideal for paddling and plundering. The glen opened out on to the long grass, and then the pebbles and sand of the beach, with nothing else there but the cove and a small wooden jetty. It was beautiful. The hills of Port Kipneash watched over them as Percy and Nell wiled away sunshine hours on Jetty Beach, collecting pebbles, searching out shells, scavenging the rockpools for crustaceous booty. They could almost call it their own.

If Percy had been listening as he and his mam made their way through the glen, he would have heard the panting breathlessness of his usually fit mother, struggling to keep apace. If he had watched, he would have seen the five or six times her legs buckled beneath her as she stumbled gracelessly through the trees. If he had looked closely, he would have seen her chattering teeth, her twitching skin.

'Laters!' he shouted as he jumped off the jetty and swam furiously, trying to make it as fast as he could to the wrecked fishing boat. It was the place he always returned to, his home from home. The wreckage lay on the seabed at the edge of the bay, at the precise point where the protection of the cove opened up into the open sea. It took minutes to swim there from the shore, but it felt like another world. He needed to see it, to feel reassured that his underwater life was still within reach, despite September seeing the return of school. He needed to make sure that the wreckage was still there, untouched, that nothing had changed.

The sea was bracing; it felt colder than it had yesterday, the night chill was already in the air and the autumn breezes were waiting just around the corner. When Percy swam, he was aware of everything around him. It was as if his body was equipped with multiple sensors that could detect danger from every angle. He would know if a large fish or a boat had entered the territory just by the change in behaviour of the small fish, or a change in the way the water was pushing up against his body. He knew if the currents were taking him too far from home because the tiniest, most miniscule change in temperature sent an electric jolt down his spine like a message from the ocean.

The boat wreck was a small fishing tug; it had become battered and broken by the sea after being left tethered to the jetty for as long as anyone could remember. The ropes had withered to thread and it had eventually drifted, hit the rock off the headland, and sunk. No one knew who it belonged to, so it belonged to the sea. It had become more than just an abandoned old boat. It was home to hundreds, maybe thousands, of sea creatures. It was Percy's hideaway.

The wreck, being at the very tip of the headland, was the last point before the cove of the little beach opened up into the wide open sea. Barnacles, mussels, shoals of tiny anchovies and herring occupied every surface and crevice. Sometimes there were bull huss and tope. The conger eels stayed away, and Percy was glad of that. They were the ugliest fish he had encountered so far and they gave him the heebie-jeebies. They were a bad omen. He never enjoyed a swim once he had seen a conger eel in the water.

Percy's hand brushed over the limpets that clung to the sides of the boat. It looked alive, the boat, covered in a grey living skin, with anemones swaying and moving all over it. The porpoises were there today with their flat teeth and flat fins. They smiled and somersaulted about him.

A massive shoal of pilchards with their baby sardines, a hurricane of them, jetted by. The collective force of the tiny fish shoved Percy away from the wreckage, and he grabbed at the rotting wood of the boat to pull himself back towards its skeleton remains. He positioned himself in his favourite nook and took in all that was around him. He felt like there were hundreds of little eyes looking back at him. When he looked around, a tail would sway away, a tentacle would out-stretch and then release out of sight. He watched a sea anemone, bright pink and blue, move with the calm of the sea, seeming to breathe in and out; without consciously trying, his own breathing did the same.

The wreck was where Percy's turtle had set up camp for most of the summer. He was gone now, though. Of course, he wasn't really Percy's turtle, he was allowed to disappear, to find another home. It didn't stop Percy missing him though.

Percy was wondering about the turtle, trying not to take the turtle's nomadic life as a personal insult, when he realised quite suddenly that his mother was not behind him. He shone his torch all around, but there was no sign. He was used to feeling her there, even if she was twenty metres away, giving him some space to explore, or basking in the warmer waters higher up. But he could not detect her at all. Something was amiss.

He felt the forceful shove of an artificial current made by a speedboat, it made him unsteady and he immediately worried for his mother. He began to panic. Thinking she was there, and then realising she was not, made him fearful. He froze. Should he swim home? Should he scream? Underwater screaming was never that useful, in his experience. What about flashing his torch on and off? What about—

He saw her, trailing slowly behind him. Her legs beat the water sluggishly, she was drifting upwards, unable to keep her own ballast.

It was unlike Mam to swim so slowly and to be so unsteady. Her face looked pained. Her legs only gave the smallest of kicks as she trod water, indicating to Percy that she would go no further tonight.

Percy didn't fight it. He nodded, and they swam home.

They walked back to the house slowly and in silence until they reached the door. Dina turned to her son and said, 'I was tired tonight because I went for a long swim while you were at school.'

Her long hair was covering her gills and it occurred to Percy that he had not seen them for some time; they were always hidden by a scarf or by her hair.

He wondered, for the first time in his life, whether his mother might not be telling him the whole truth.

Chapter 5

Remember the Scuba

NELL

Nell stroked her neck and silently cursed the day that nature picked her twin brother to be one of its wonders, and not her.

Dina stepped quietly into Nell's bedroom.

'I thought you were out with *the boys*,' grumbled Nell.

'Not today. They don't need me so much now,' said Dina. She sounded tired.

'This'll be the sixth day in a row.'

'I know. But it's good that Percy has a gilly friend. You understand that, don't you?'

Nell nodded. She understood. And she had been happy for Percy. But things had changed. There was nothing innately annoying about Connor. He seemed OK. And Nell was getting used to having him around. But she couldn't imagine ever being his *friend*. He was Percy's friend. If anything, she was vaguely irritated by his constant presence. Irritated and, if she was honest, a little jealous too.

'Dad's got a motor on the table, he'll be getting grease everywhere,' Nell growled. Finding fault with everyone else wasn't making her feel any less lonely.

'I know. I don't have the energy to be cross today, my love.' Dina smiled her soft smile. 'Let's go out. You and me.'

'Really?'

'Why not.' Dina smiled again. 'Remember the scuba?' she said, before she left Nell to get ready for their swim. 'Don't face your frustrations alone.'

Remember the scuba.

Less a question than a command. *Remember it.*

* * *

It had been generally accepted that Dina and Goldie's decision to enrol their seven-year-old daughter in thrice-weekly scuba diving lessons was an unusual decision to make. But to the Shearwater family, it made complete sense. Nell was not a gilly, but her twin brother was. She was so desperate to be like Percy, that she was taking more and more risks with her swimming. She had begun to swim too deep in an attempt to keep up with her brother. She had, more than once, raced out with a snorkel and flippers and made her way to the edge of the bay before Goldie could catch up with her. It was only a matter of time before she completely lost sight of her limitations and put herself in real danger.

The diving school had said no to begin with. There was no chance a child under ten would be able to reach the required level of understanding and maturity. No chance. But when the diving school finally relented, it only took six weeks for her to prove everyone wrong. At seven years old she was the best student they had ever had, regardless of her age.

It had started as a great day, the day she earned her diving certificate and her very own scuba gear. Finally, she was allowed out into the open sea and it felt like the start of a new chapter.

But nothing changed. Not really.

She'd spent the entire day having the same battles as always. Her tank got heavy after a while, her flippers were either too tight or too loose, and her oxygen would not last forever. Goldie put her on strict rations. Nothing she did could make her swim like Percy. And because of the tank, she couldn't keep up with Percy or swim into the nooks and crannies he explored with ease. It was a cold day, too cold for March, the winds were up and her body became tired quickly. Percy had grown frustrated too, once the novelty of Nell being there had worn off.

'It's day one, Nelly, give it time,' Goldie had reassured her. But Nell felt defeated.

While everyone was asleep that night, Nell had crept out of the house in her wet suit. Her coat was wrapped tightly around her shoulders, but nothing could stop the cruel bite of frost in the air.

She'd walked to the edge of the shore, the moon looking down on her with a cold glow of disapproval. 'What are you looking at?' she'd responded with a determined frown. She took off her coat and stood, shivering, at the sea's beckoning edge, the cold waves lapping at her ankles. Seaweed curled itself around her toes and the stones felt sharp under her feet. She hadn't brought her damn flippers. She'd left behind her all-important (and, to her mind, completely stupid) self-contained underwater breathing apparatus: her scuba gear. It was just her and the sea.

The rest of that night was a blur. There were certain things she could remember with vivid clarity. But there were some things that her mind had blocked out forever too.

She could still remember standing under the one lonely lamp which lit up the jetty with just enough light for Nell to see a few metres around her. Mam's feet were webbed and like rubber, hard and shiny through years of sea-walking. Nell could remember her own soft feet feeling cold and sore. She'd wanted to run in, she'd willed her body to do it. 'Move!' she grumbled through gritted and chattering teeth. But she was glued to the spot.

Then she was in the sea up to her waist. The water was jerking and jolting her, calling her in.

Then it was up to her neck, the sea moving her slowly this way and that, but her body knew better and her feet were fixed, steadfast, to the spot. Staring at the vast open sea, she'd screamed wildly and it had felt like the sea was screaming back. The sea had chosen the wrong child. It should have been her.

She could still feel the pull of the waves and the fight for breath. She could still conjure the feel of the sea bed on her fingertips and the sensation of wondering which way was up. She remembered hitting her head, not knowing how far out she was, and that she was completely, totally alone. She remembered the dark, dark sea.

She'd woken up on the beach, to the sound of Mam's screams and the squawks of frantic birds as the sun began to rise. There were feathers all around her.

In the ambulance, the shaking would not stop. As she had drifted in and out of life, she'd heard familiar voices, and unfamiliar voices. Someone said the word 'hypothermia'. Mam was alternating wails with sobs. Goldie kept telling her it would be OK. He said it so many times it began to sound like he didn't really believe it.

The doctor had called it convalescence, that time spent at first in the hospital and then in bed or in front of the fire at home. But to Nell, they were just long words for boredom.

Dina had brought her a book to draw pictures in, of things she saw during the long hours looking out of the window or into the fire, and soon the book was full, but the pictures were never of things that anyone else could see.

'What have you drawn today, Nell? Do you want to show me?' Goldie had asked one night as he tucked her in to bed.

The pictures were wonderful, intricate imaginings of people and objects and places that surely Nell had only encountered in her dreams.

'Where did you get these images, Nelly?'

'What do you mean?' she'd asked, confused. They felt so real to her. The idea that she had *got* them felt wrong. They just existed.

'You must have copied them from somewhere, surely?'

'No. I just see them, here.' Little Nell had touched her forehead and Goldie had smiled. He bent down and kissed her head.

'You're drawing from your mind's eye, that's right.' His eyes were warm and his face had creased with his smile. 'Well, I would certainly take that power over gills any day of the week.'

* * *

If Nell hadn't accepted it before that night, she certainly did afterwards: she was not a gilly and she would never experience what it was like to be a gilly, no matter how hard she battled with it in her own room, or in her own head. That's what Mam meant when she told her to remember the scuba. Nell had a tendency to battle things alone, even if the battle was a losing one.

But drawing was different. Drawing was like dreaming; it felt easy for Nell. It was second nature, like a warm blanket. She never had to try that hard when it came to her pictures. It felt like a power. Pictures just flowed from her like a river to the sea.

Nell looked out of the window. Mam was stood outside the front door, clipping the dead heads off the roses so that they'd grow again, stronger. She was waiting for her daughter to swim with her. Nell smiled and rushed downstairs to grab her wet suit and to run to the sea.

Chapter 6

The Sea

NELL

Nell heaved on her wet suit and her tank and got ready to dive.

Her feet hung off the side of the *Queen Mab* as it waited in dock, bobbing gently in the slow throb of the sea.

The *Queen Mab* was a small yacht with a motor. It had two ragged and patched-up sails that Nell knew irritated her father. *I must get round to those sails*, he would mutter every time they climbed aboard. But Goldie had neither the money nor the time to tend to the boat like he wanted to. He was always

53

busy fixing things for other people; rarely did he have time to fix anything for himself. That was his job after all: clocks and engines, toasters and televisions. If something was broken, Goldie Shearwater would fix it. 'Goldie' happened to be the name given to him by his parents, but it was also a name that suited him to the core. Goldie always made things that were broken *shine*, like gold. Maybe that's why neither Percy nor Nell felt compelled to call him 'dad' – it didn't seem enough. The name Goldie suited him, it felt much more appropriate.

Goldie would call the *Mab* 'the family yacht, don't-you-know', and the twins would roll their eyes. The paint was flaky and faded, and the fabric on the benches was worn with great holes and patches.

Nell could hear Goldie below deck. He was whistling, which meant he must be feeling seasick – it was his remedy. The science was shaky at best.

Jetty Beach was still in view and everything felt familiar, yet different. Mam seemed different. Nell watched Mam rub her eyes and breathe deeply as she looked up at the sky. They both soaked in the freshness of the air. Nell felt the urge to check on Mam, to make sure she was ready. Then they jumped, together.

Mam's eyes were wide and shone in the sea, crystal-like. Nell resisted fiddling with her mask, but it felt uncomfortable and made her nose itch. The cloud of tiny bubbles made by their dive tangled with the bubbles made by the swish of a grey seal as it sped gracefully past.

Nell and Dina headed for the sea bed. It was thick with seagrass, anemones, crustaceans, beautiful colour and vibrant life. Dina settled herself next to a rock and let it all move around her, amidst the sway of the water and the gentle nudge of the currents. Nell struggled to stop herself from drifting; her body wasn't made like her mother's.

A Risso's dolphin edged into their territory, hunting a cuttlefish. It spotted them and performed its show of acrobatics, somersaulting and twisting. It jerked its head up as if to invite applause. Nell felt the contractions of a laugh creep and wind through the muscles in her face, restricted as she was by her mask. Dina just smiled. This dolphin was still dark coloured. By the time of its old age it would be white with scars from fighting its own kind. It made Nell think of her mother's greying skin. She looked battle-sore.

Dina walked on the sea bed, strolling unnoticed amongst its wonders. Nell watched through her itching mask as the fish approached her mother, allowing her to hold them, not as specimens, but as friends. All Nell could do was watch, and keep as still as possible so as not to scare them off. Walking on the sea bed wasn't a right of the gillies, it was her mam's well-earned privilege. And despite all that humans had done to the sea, the sea always welcomed Dina.

I would have made a good gilly, she thought. *Better than Percy.*

As Nell sat on the deck of the *Mab*, peeling off the paraphernalia, Dina's head suddenly appeared at the edge of the boat. She looked drained, grey, tired. She was panting, out of breath. Nell took a towel to her. She hadn't seen her mam like this before.

'I'm fine, I'm all right,' Dina said, when she could, between deep breaths. Nell knew the smile on her face was a lie.

And then the smile vanished. Nell followed the line of her mother's gaze and saw that she was staring intently at a bird that had been hovering around the *Mab*.

'Oh, don't be afraid Mam, it's just a bird. In fact, I think I must have seen it before, it's in some of my drawings, I recognise—'

'It's a razorbill,' interrupted Dina. She climbed aboard, and held the towel closer to her body.

'All OK?' Goldie grinned as he emerged from below deck.

'It means she's on her way. She feels it. It means it's getting worse,' Dina muttered.

From the look on her mother's face, Nell knew not to ask any questions.

Chapter 7

Dina

PERCY

'I think something's wrong with Mam,' said Percy to Nell, squinting as the lowering sun shone through the window of Nell's room.

'Say it. I think I know what you're going to say. But say it,' said Nell, discarding her pencil and drawing.

'Well, don't you think she sleeps a lot more now? She stays in bed right until lunch. She doesn't eat much. And she was really weird on our swim the other day.'

Nell was silent.

'She's started hiding her gills,' whispered Percy.

'Grub's up, you two!' came a call up the stairs. It was Goldie. It didn't matter that he had been interrupted, Percy could see in his sister's eyes that she already knew what he was saying.

Percy could smell the deep and familiar smell of Goldie's beetroot soup. Just the right amount of vinegar. It was a delicate balance. The twins made their way downstairs. The table was set with spoons and bowls, a loaf sliced unevenly and the fire burning hard with flames charging and curling at the burner's windows. There was a platter of rollmop herrings and cheese too. Percy rubbed his chin to check he hadn't dribbled, the food looked and smelled so good.

'Are you OK, Mam?' asked Nell. Dina was shivering as her feet touched the cold tiled floor. Goldie put his arm around her waist and seemed to pull her in for a kiss on the cheek as usual. But it wasn't an embrace. He was helping her to stand straight.

Dina sat down at the table and her wide smile returned. 'I'm not poorly. I'm OK. Just a little tired at the moment. So Grannie Marnie is going to come and stay while I get back to my usual self.'

'So you will, you know, get better?' said Percy.

'Of course! I have a virus, the kind that goes around and everyone gets. But, I need to look after myself better... get some rest. I'm afraid, Percy, I won't be able to swim with you as often as we usually do. But Connor's father is home for a few days and he has said that he will go with you, and, well, you can go out whenever you like with Connor now.'

'So, you're OK?' asked Nell again. Percy watched his sister look deep into their mother's eyes, as if Nell had a power to see what Mam was really thinking. Nell frowned as she looked for the truth.

'I will be, little one. I will be.'

Percy didn't think this was a lie, but he wasn't sure that it was the truth either.

Chapter 8

Marnie

PERCY

There were three knocks. A velvety voice, low but certainly female, sang, '*Ho-laaaa!*' through the letterbox.

'Who's that?' said Nell, standing on the stairs with Percy close behind.

Goldie opened the door and there, with big curler-curls and bright red lips that held a wide, certain smile, was Granny Marnie. Her cheeks were painted-on pink, almost purple, and her eyes were decorated with a thick black line all around them like a pharaoh. She wore a long, luxurious woollen coat that grazed the floor. It was camel-coloured and its thick, luscious collar looked like the regal mane of a proud lion.

'Mama, you came,' said Dina, smiling with apprehensive joy.

'Surely you always knew I'd be here, *guapa*?' said Marnie with authority and a wide smile, her cat-like eyes shining by the dim light of the Shearwater home. 'Ten years!'

'Twelve, Marnie, it's been twelve years now,' Goldie made a point of saying, as he leant down to kiss her on the cheek. 'We've missed you.'

'Really? That long? My goodness, the cure for a broken heart is so *very* hard to find.' Marnie shook her head gently and stared at the floor for a moment. 'London, Paris, the Amazon, Madagascar – even Antarctica, I've been *everywhere*. But I always promised to return, no?'

Goldie picked up Marnie's giant trunk and brought it into the house. 'Looks like she's staying for a while then,' grumbled Percy quietly as he and Nell watched on from their perch at the top of the stairs.

'Well, I do suspect that you already *knew* I was on my way. I believe you had a visit from my friend?' Marnie turned to Dina, staring into her daughter's eyes.

'She's *intense*,' whispered Nell to her brother.

Percy nodded in agreement.

'I like it,' whispered Nell. Percy watched his sister gazing at the old woman – she had a delight in her eyes that confused him. 'She looks like a movie star or something.'

'Yes, I saw the razorbill, mother,' Dina sighed.

Marnie stepped further into the house, and stooped as if the ceiling was only millimetres above her head. She regally observed each corner of the Shearwater's small home. 'Well, it's not the *Ritz de Paris* but it will do, *chica*. How *are* we?' She looked at her daughter. Her dark, arched eyebrows rose up to the middle of her forehead and in one dramatic move, her arms shot out from her elbows as if propelled by electricity, and she flung herself around Dina's neck. '*Ma corazon!*' she cried.

Percy looked down at Goldie for reassurance, perplexed by Marnie's exuberance and worried that she appeared to be having some sort of seizure. *My heart*, mouthed Goldie in translation, as he beckoned them down the stairs.

'Is she having a heart attack?' said Percy, plodding down the stairs.

Nell chuckled. 'She's being *emotional*, Percy.'

Dina managed to release herself from her mother's grip. She turned to her bewildered family. 'Grandma is fine. I think she needs a cup of tea.'

'*Grandma*?' exclaimed Marnie, confusion in her eyes. 'Ah, yes! Why, of course! Grandma! *Abuela*...' She shook her head. 'Where are they? Where are my *grandchildren*?' The word seemed to jar, it was stuck in her mouth and came out sounding like a word from a foreign tongue. She surveyed the room, not able at first to see what was right in front of her eyes. 'There you are, my sweet, sweet darlings!' she glided over to the twins and smothered them with big, wet red-lipped kisses.

'*Besos! Besos! Besos!* What a celebration it is to see you now after this longest of times.'

'Marnie, would you like a—' began Goldie.

'Yes! A cup of chai! Yes! *Buena idea!*'

And as Goldie brewed the tea, and Dina and Marnie sat by the fire, Nell and Percy stood in stunned silence as their eyes were drawn like the pull of the moon to a dark shadow in the window. Nell held tightly to her brother's arm, the tips of her fingers turning white, but Percy didn't push her away.

'What is that? Do you see it too?' whispered Percy.

64

A flash of bright white, and two shining dot eyes burned at them through the glass of the window.

'I see it. I've seen it before. It was on the *Mab*, it's a razor-bill. I think it's Marnie's bird.'

It stared right at them.

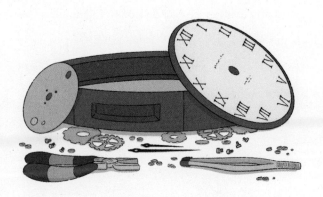

Chapter 9

What to Make of Marnie

NELL

When Grandma Marnie came to stay, she brought with her sufficient supplies to last a month. After two days she called for more and declared that she would be staying at least until the spring. September had barely ended. March was five months away.

And then, October turned from green to red in the blink of an eye. The living light of the yellow sun turned to the wilting yellow of the dying leaves, and November was knocking.

Nell watched Marnie like a museum piece. She was not like a rough dug-up relic, with sharp edges of stone worn down by time in the grub of the earth. She was more like a delicate jewel, its elegance faded by time. A jewel that had been worn too much, cared for too much.

She didn't walk, she glided. She didn't move around the kitchen like Goldie, she floated, she pirouetted. Nell crept wide-eyed up the stairs after school, her back to the wall, as Marnie sang melancholy French ballads while she cleaned the kitchen dressed in diamanté and wearing curlers. Nell hid behind the pantry wall to watch her grandmother as she concocted mysterious dinners with the flair of a Parisian chef. She had taken over the cooking as much as she had taken over the house. And she liked to cook small. Very small indeed.

Things were no different when Connor came round after school. 'Don't worry,' whispered Percy to his friend who was gawping at the plate in front of him. 'I have crackers in my room.'

'What is it?' murmured Connor, unused to the spectacle that was Marnie's cuisine.

'Cottage pie,' groaned Nell, prodding her fork at the small squashed potato, six peas and a single cube of braised steak that adorned her plate.

'Wow,' said Connor, bemused.

'Tell me about it.' Percy shook his head.

Marnie spent hours in the kitchen, using every cooking instrument available, every pot and pan. She assembled delicate and intricate dishes covered with a 'jus' or a 'foam', with a sprig of something from the garden, sometimes a flower, placed delicately on the side of the plate. After dinner, Goldie and the twins would hide in the pantry wolfing down bread and milk so that they didn't go to bed on an empty stomach.

Nell had begun to see a goodness in Marnie that Percy was blind to. How was he supposed to see it when he was always out with Connor?

'If you spent a bit more time at home you'd see Marnie's pretty interesting, actually,' Nell said to Percy one morning on the walk to school.

'It's not my fault I'm gilly. You do realise I *have* to go out to the sea. And you could join us you know – bring your scuba gear.'

Nell rolled her eyes and shook her head. 'It's not the same now Connor's *always* around.'

'Your choice. Anyway, who says I don't see that Marnie's interesting? I see it. I mean, she's also a bit weird, though.'

'That's what I like. At least she's not boring. She's eccentric. I like it.'

'Well, I think *you're* eccentric,' smirked Percy.

When no one was around, Nell would sneak into the cupboard under the stairs and wrap herself in Marnie's long lion coat. It smelled sweet and delicious, and it felt strangely safe.

But there were questions too.

'Isn't it weird that she never wanted to visit us before?' Nell asked Goldie, cradling her chin in her hands and resting her head on her elbows as she watched him perform the delicate art of putting a clock back together.

Goldie looked up and his head torch shone in her eyes, making her wince. He had been fiddling with the same tiny bit of brass spring-wire for nearly an hour and was getting tetchy.

'What?' he growled, uncharacteristically irritated.

'I thought clocks were your favourite?' Nell retorted. '"A palimpsest" you said. "You can see decades in the shadows of time" you said,' she grumbled defensively.

Goldie took every opportunity to explain to his children that a palimpsest was perfectly imperfect, just like life often is. A palimpsest could be a scroll, a piece of paper, parchment, a chalk board – anything where the previous owner's scribing could still be seen beneath the new owner's work. Clocks were like that. Goldie could see the layers of repair carried out over the years. Goldie didn't like new things. He adored unearthing the scars of the past.

Goldie put the spring down and looked at his girl.

'What is it, Nell? What's bothering you now?'

'Why did Marnie never visit us before?'

'It's a good question. It's... yes... it's a valid question.'

'Well?' said Nell, impatiently.

'Well. Yes. It's hard to explain.'

'Have a go,' goaded Nell, intolerant of her father's inability to get straight to the point.

'Your grandad—'

'Fynlo?'

'Yes, Fynlo. He had to leave, and Marnie had... erm...' Goldie looked uncomfortable. 'She had, well, I guess she had a lot of emotions to deal with.'

If Percy had been there, he would have puffed out his cheeks and pretended to vomit.

'Why did he leave, then?' asked Nell.

'Your grandad helped to build the *Monabeg*, you know that, don't you?'

'Yes, but what's that got to do with it?' asked Nell, confused.

'Uh, well...' Goldie was grappling for the right words.

A whisper came from the fire. 'Goldie, that is enough.'

Goldie looked over to his stirring wife, then back at Nell. 'Nelly, I need to get this finished for Mr Hamble.'

'Did he get lost at sea?' Nell continued.

'Who, Nelly?' sighed Goldie, with his full attention back on the tiny spring that he held gently between his fingers.

'Fynlo. Did he get lost at sea?'

'No. Nell, haven't we talked about this before?' complained Goldie. 'Look, it's hard to explain. Gillies have to make decisions that the rest of us don't have to think about, and those decisions have consequences, OK?'

'I get it.' Nell knew when to stop.

But she did not get it. She did not get it at all. She had more questions.

Where had Marnie been?

Why was she here now?

Where was Fynlo?

And, perhaps the most confounding question of all, why did the razorbill keep appearing at her bedroom window?

Chapter 10

Percy Learns of Doona

PERCY

Percy could not sleep. He climbed out of his bed in a dazed stupor, made worse by the fact that he'd been lying wide awake, sheep-counting, for what felt like hours.

He crept towards the stairs, heading for the kitchen, hoping a snack might settle him into sleep. But as he began to make his way down the creaky stairs, he stopped himself from going further. Goldie and Dina were still awake, and they were talking in low voices with the glow of the fire lighting up their faces.

Percy sat on the stairs in darkness, and listened as his parents talked. He got the feeling that this quiet conversation was not something he should be listening to, which only made him listen harder.

'She came just at the right time, didn't she?' said Mam. 'Of course she knew I was getting worse. She has eyes everywhere. The birds are always watching.'

'She's driving Percy mad with the food situation though.' Goldie had a lightness in his voice that sounded like a smile.

'Poor Percy. He must be starving after his swims.'

'He'll get over it. We have snack-parties in the pantry cupboard, he's fine.'

Percy frowned in silent disagreement as his parents laughed. Marnie's portion sizes were no laughing matter as far as he was concerned. He carried on listening to them, careful not to make a sound.

'I need to do something, Goldie. I can't carry on like this. Things could get a lot worse, and very quickly. I still have hope that I can fight it, but I can't just wait for this weakness to take hold completely. I have to do something while I still can.'

'The Indian Ocean. We could go, all of us – we'd never need to come back,' whispered Goldie.

'Come on, Goldie, you know very well that I can't leave Kipneash, not forever. I am the last Gatekeeper of Doona. We can't risk the gateway from Kipneash to Doona being exposed.'

A shiver of hot electricity shot down Percy's spine, the hairs on his arms prickled.

Doona.

He had never heard that word before, but it felt so familiar.

'If your father knew...'

'I know what you are going to say. That I should go to him. That I should go to Doona. But I can't swim that far now, I'm too weak. I'd never find it. I would never feel *the pull* in this condition.' Dina looked down at her exhausted, wilting frame, draped in blankets and limp.

'I would find it for you.' Goldie took her hands and clasped them in his.

'You know that's impossible,' breathed Dina heavily. 'It is too much of a risk for us all to go, and I would never leave you and the children, anyway. I've spent my entire life being the Gatekeeper. My role is to *stop* people from going to Doona. It would be hypocritical... If I went there I would never be able to return. It would be no place for the children even if we were all to go – they need normality, they need a normal life.'

75

'Doona is the only place on this earth where you would be guaranteed perfect balance. The last unspoiled place. Where gillies came from, where the world can meet your needs. We have to at least *try*. When we got married, I took the Shearwater name, and I was proud to,' said Goldie, barely audible now. Percy leant in, shuffling down to the next stair. 'Shearwaters don't give up. I may not be a gilly, but I am a Shearwater, and I will never give up. I know we could make it to Doona.' The desperation in his father's voice frightened Percy.

'Oh, Goldie. Why don't you understand? I am only here in Kipneash to protect the gateway to Doona. The Shearwaters have always been Gatekeepers. I may not be much use right now, but I have so much training to do with Percy.'

'I do understand.' Goldie paused, the room was still. 'I hate to say it, Dina, but times have changed. Being a Gatekeeper is not what it once was. The crew of the *Monabeg* can quite easily perform the job without your help. How long has it been since an alarm was raised? How long has it been since you were required to perform your duty?' Silence echoed in the room. '*Years*. It has been *years*, Dina.' Goldie answered his own question. 'It would not be negligent for you to leave. And it certainly would not be hypocritical for *you* go to Doona.

You of all people would never do it any harm.' Goldie's eyes grew wider as he pleaded with her. 'What if your father could give you part of the tree, to bring home? If you can't go there to live, maybe we could go there and bring a part of Doona back here?'

'Don't even suggest such a thing! You can't take things from Doona, you know that! And if anyone found out about it, the power of it... People are greedy. All that's good about Doona would be turned bad, it would be corrupted. Some things aren't supposed to be touched by human hands. You *know* this, Goldie,' Dina scolded her husband. Percy didn't often hear his mother's angry voice, but it was fearsome. 'If anyone knew that we had even a leaf from that tree it would cause chaos. People would try to turn it into money, into wealth, they'd destroy everything that is good about it. What grows in Doona must remain in Doona. Always.'

Percy watched as his mother shuffled in her seat, trying to get comfortable.

'I am already too weak to make that journey. I no longer feel *the pull* at all. Please, no more talk of it,' Dina let out a long sigh and rubbed her forehead.

'You're tired,' said Goldie as he held Dina's hand. 'I'm sorry.'

Both adults sat in silence for several minutes. Percy fought the thing in his stomach which was telling him to call out. To wrap his arms around his tired, sad mother. To demand answers.

Finally, Dina broke the silence.

'He's not ready yet. He's not even nearly ready. *The pull* could overpower him. Percy mustn't know about Doona. Don't breathe a word of that place.'

Goldie paused.

'Promise me, now, Goldie!'

'I promise! I promise.'

But it was too late.

Chapter 11

Unwilling Ears

PERCY

'Not now!' Nell grunted as she pushed her way past Percy and charged down the stairs. He followed at a normal pace. 'I'm walking to school with Sadie. Got to meet her at quarter-past, don't want to be late.'

Percy had tried to tell Nell about Doona several times that morning, but whenever he glimpsed an opportunity, Goldie would suddenly appear, or Marnie would pop out from nowhere. The news was bubbling inside him like a volcano ready to erupt.

As Goldie served up bowls of porridge, Percy grabbed his sister by the cardigan and pulled her out of the house, easing the door closed behind them. Percy stammered, fighting to get the words out.

'Percy! Look at my feet, my slippers are wet now! This is ridiculous. Dad!' Nell shouted, tugging herself away from his grip.

Before Percy could even get a single word out, Marnie popped her head around the front door and Nell shot back inside.

'First frost? *Que bonita!* So pretty! Come out to look at it, have you? Good work, my lovely ones. Now, come inside, your breakfast is ready! *Pronto!*'

Percy was so frustrated he made a dent in the table with his spoon by grinding it down so hard. Thankfully no one noticed. For everyone else, life was going on the same as usual. But for Percy, things were happening in slow motion; everything around him felt blurred and secondary, like it was taking place in the background of a painting. The only thing at the front of his mind was Doona.

And at school it was no different.

In the classroom it was test day; they were all sitting on individual tables trying to fathom decimals and division. He looked at Connor, who was hunched over his work, scribbling away, working out answers and checking he wasn't wrong. Percy tried to concentrate on his own work, but his mind was full of bigger things. Mrs Angkor wore her impenetrable veneer of disapproval; she was not tolerating any funny business today. There was no way he would get to speak to Nell in the classroom, and anyway, he couldn't risk anyone hearing.

The longer he waited to tell Nell about what he had heard, the more muddled it all became. He needed to let the words out before they took on a life of their own.

At the end of school, Percy grabbed hold of his sister, and again she pulled away.

'What are you doing? I've got street dance!' she shouted, annoyed, as she ran off. Percy huffed. But instead of walking home he waited in the school library for Nell.

He couldn't even read a book, his mind was so full of thoughts creeping into every nook and cranny of his brain. When Nell finally emerged from street dance in her tracksuit, Percy let out an audible sigh of relief. 'Finally,' he muttered under his breath as Nell said goodbye to her friends. 'Now, Nelly, I need to speak to you, *now!*' he demanded as they made their way to the school gate, alone at last.

But then, like the punchline to an extremely unfunny joke, Marnie turned up to walk home with them.

'Marnie, what are you doing here?' said Nell.

'I thought we could take the *Queen Mab* for a sail, just us. The sky is clear, the air is chilled and it's still light – I'd say we have less than an hour until it's black.'

Chapter 12

The Pull

PERCY

While Marnie was on the deck of the *Mab*, and he and Nell were below, Percy seized his chance.

Percy told Nell everything he could remember. He described the scene and how serious their mother and father had looked. He told her about Fynlo and Doona, and that there was something there that might help Mam – a tree. He couldn't slow down, the words tumbled over each other like a wave crashing against the lighthouse walls.

'Doola?' mumbled Nell, unconvinced.

'No, *Doona*. Doona! It's a place. Listen properly! They didn't say a lot, but from what they did say... I think it's Mam's best hope. It's—'

'Thick as thieves!' interrupted Marnie, smirking with dark delight as if she had caught a jackal in the act. She glided so slowly and smoothly down the steps into the cabin of the *Mab* that Percy wondered if he should check that her feet were even touching the floor. 'You do realise that I can hear *every* word you are saying down here?' Her eyes seemed to be half-closed, squinting into Percy's soul. Maybe it was the way she wore the heavy black make-up around her eyes, but he felt sure that he could feel the touch of her stare on his reddening cheeks.

'Well, seeing as you know *all about* Doona – which, by the way, you *don't* – I may as well tell you a few *basic* rules, *chicos*. A seed of knowledge has been planted and, although your mother might never forgive me for telling you, there is a very real danger that from that metaphorical seed an unruly plant will grow. The last thing we need is for that plant to become infested with parasites, or overrun with weeds! It befalls me, I suppose, to ensure it receives the necessary nutrients,' she said, coolly. 'And is adequately

84

pruned.' She stared at Percy as she made a cutting motion with her fingers.

Percy's eyes widened.

'*Primero!*' shouted Marnie, raising a single finger and sitting down on the banquette next to Nell. 'You won't find Doona on a map, oh no. They say gillies have an instinct that draws them there. *The pull.* Doona is the gilly habitat as it was *meant* to be, as *the world* was meant to be. Only there can gillies live in perfect balance. *Perfecto.*'

Percy pictured Connor on that first day of school, and how Dina looked now, frail in front of the fire – both like they were not meant for this world. For Dina it had been a slow process; there had been too many coughs and colds, an infection in her gills last year that she couldn't shift, too much pressure on her weakening body, too many winters away from the warmer seas of the Indian Ocean. Each of Dina's ailments was like a drop of water into a cup that was now beginning to overflow.

For Connor it was different. Weakness hadn't crept up on him, it had always been there. The weakness in his left gill meant that he would always struggle to find balance, he would always have to fight to be strong.

Percy was lucky, he knew that. But he didn't know how long his luck would last. Finding balance was like walking a tightrope. It was so easy to fall. Too easy.

'However,' Marnie continued, 'Doona, like all rare treasures, is deeply, deeply vulnerable. It is a treasure that would be plundered in a second, if the wrong people were given the chance.' Marnie closed her eyes and took a deep breath. 'At the heart of Doona, there is a tree. A very precious tree. People say that it contains in its sap the life blood of the earth, the purest elixir.'

'An elixir that could restore a gilly's balance, if it has been lost?' Percy hung on to every one of Marnie's words.

'Yes, that is what they say.' Marnie nodded. 'But people have other reasons to go there. Corrupt reasons.'

'What do you mean?' asked Nell.

'It is unknown what else that elixir could achieve. Someone tried to find out once. They tried to take it from Doona. They tried to steal from that precious tree and the repercussions were devastating.' Percy strained to hear as Marnie closed her eyes, shook her head and muttered what sounded like a name. Before Percy could ask Marnie to repeat herself, she began speaking again, hastily and angrily. 'As residents of this planet, we *all* benefit from Doona and the goodness of that tree. Doona and the tree – they cannot belong to any *one* person, they cannot be *owned*. People only see what the tree can do for them, and not what it does for our planet. It makes me so cross! It is because of that very tree that the rolling hills of this island still shine emerald green, and the skies above Kipneash are crystal blue, despite the horrors that mankind has inflicted on our beautiful planet. And don't get me started on what the oceans would be without Doona's nourishment! Left to man alone, the seas would be a mire of decay, all life suffocated!' Marnie shuddered.

'But Marnie, this all sounds like folklore, it can't possibly be true, can it?' Nell pulled her cardigan around her shoulders.

The *Mab* felt cold all of a sudden and Percy felt a shiver rush down his spine and into his legs.

'Most people would agree with you, *chica*. And I have no quibble there. Let the doubters doubt if it means they will leave Doona alone!' Marnie smiled. 'Over many years of flux and change, and many failed attempts at reaching its hallowed shores, talk of Doona has faded. And thankfully so. But it is different for gillies. My Fynlo believes the tree is a spirit; he thought he could hear it talking to him. He said that *the pull* is the call of the tree and only gillies can hear it.'

'The pull?' whispered Nell. 'Do you feel it... this *pull*, Percy?'

Percy shrugged, not sure what to say.

'If you do, dear boy, you must ignore it! Don't listen to those thoughts. There have been many tragedies. *Many*. The sea in the Doona core ring is unlike any other sea, it baffles anyone who swims or sails in its waters. The route is completely uncharted, traditional methods of navigation are redundant, and they say there is a curse that will get you if the sea does not. You know what a core ring is, don't you?'

The children shook their heads blankly.

'It's a ring of water, warmer or colder than the rest, that breaks off from the usual circulation of the ocean,' explained Marnie. 'It breaks off from the current. The striking thing about the Doona core ring is that it is always there, it never moves, and yet it is virtually impossible to cross. Unless you know how to cheat it.' Marnie blinked twice and cleared her throat before continuing. 'A lot of fishermen around here are superstitious about it. They would never venture that way, just to be safe.'

'What's so dangerous about it? I mean, isn't it just another current?' asked Percy. Percy didn't fear currents; he was an expert in reading the sea and avoiding dangerous waters.

'No. It's different. The gateway to the core ring is surrounded by eddies. Anyone in search of Doona would have to navigate through the eddies, miles and miles wide. They are horridly violent whirlpools with no way around them; they have to be traversed, you must go *through* them to get into the Doona core ring. The eddies put most people off. Have you ever swum in an eddy, my boy? No? It's not easy. In fact, it's treacherous. Deadly. The swells! Did you know that there can be cyclones *under* the water in the North Atlantic Drift? It would be enough to send you mad!'

'I'm sorry Marnie, I just don't buy it,' said Nell defiantly.

There wasn't a shred of doubt in Percy's mind. He, unlike his sister, believed that everything Marnie was telling them was true.

Marnie gently stroked her curls. She cinched in her coat around her waist and cleared her throat, tilting her nose to the ceiling of the cabin before continuing.

'Believe me, Nell, I know about Doona. Not many do. But *I* do. I have my spies.' An image of the razorbill flashed into Percy's mind, the white stripe on its beak like a shot across the night.

'It just sounds so much like...' Nell hesitated. 'Like a myth.'

Percy glared at his sister. Thoughts were spinning around his head, filling his mind with questions and possibilities, but Nell just shrugged.

'A myth it most certainly is not!' replied Marnie, incensed. 'Where were we? Ah, that's right, *segundo!*' Marnie turned to Percy and whispered, 'that means *secondly*, my sweet.'

Nell sniggered.

Percy didn't care, he was used to being underestimated.

'You must not tell *anyone* about Doona.' Marnie said this sternly, as if giving a command to an unruly dog. 'The fewer who know about Doona, the better. Gillies and non-gillies alike.'

'I won't tell anyone,' promised Percy. 'But Connor must know about it already. I bet he does. I mean, his dad worked on the *Cousteau*. He's bound to know about Doona.'

'No! No, no, no! If Connor does not already know about Doona, it cannot be *you* who informs him. He may start to feel *the pull*. It cannot be risked. He must not be told until those who know him best, his *family*, are ready to tell him. I have seen the living remains of those who have tried to get there, with their broken bodies and broken souls. And they're the lucky ones,' Marnie inhaled deeply, closing her eyes, as if preparing to dive. 'There was a boy, when your mother was a child. He was your mother's only gilly friend. He had big ideas, thought he was invincible. And he was strong, *fuerte*, much stronger than your friend Connor. Michael, he was called, although your mother always called him Mica.' Percy imagined his mother as a child – it was hard to picture. 'Mica heard about Doona and *the pull* tormented him. It wouldn't let him go. He thought about it day and night, he became obsessed. He was strong, but he lacked the strength of will to resist *the pull*.'

'What did he do?' whispered Nell, suddenly interested in Marnie's story.

'He went. Tried to get your mother to go too, but she had sense enough to know her limits.'

'Did he get there?' asked Percy.

'Did he get back?' asked Nell.

'Neither,' murmured Marnie, head hung low. 'People become akin to driftwood from broken boats. Getting into the Doona core ring, through those eddies, takes a lot of skill – or a lot of luck. Neither of which he had. And say you get into the Doona core ring waters – say you do it, what then? Then you have to navigate for days, weeks even, to find your way to Doona itself. Compasses don't work. The stars don't align. It is unnavigable. Sometimes *the pull* is not enough.'

Marnie stopped, perhaps realising that she had gone too far. 'Dina is weak. As weak as I have ever seen a gilly before. The greatest hope for her lies in moving to warmer waters, different seas, the Indian Ocean. Hope does not lie in voyaging to Doona.'

'I can see mischief in your eyes, Percy,' whispered Nell as Marnie put the kettle on the stove and waited for it to boil. 'Leave it alone. Don't think about this, Percy. Leave it.'

But he would not.

'So where do they go – the gillies I mean – when they feel this *pull*?' Percy prodded. Marnie stirred a drop of milk into her tea. Now she had started to talk about Doona, she didn't seem to want to stop.

Nell gave her brother a kick under the table. 'Stop it,' she hissed. 'Leave it alone.'

Marnie gently placed her cup down on the table. 'Fynlo used to say that he could see *the pull*, like a forcefield around Kitterlund. No other gilly has ever felt *the pull* like that. Fynlo was different. You're a lot like him, Percy.'

'What has Doona got to do with Kitterlund?' asked Percy.

'Most get as far as Kitterlund. That bit isn't hard. You've been there, I'd hazard a guess?' said Marnie.

'Yes. We've been. Everyone's been. They take you on a boat with school, to look at the bird colonies,' murmured Nell.

On a clear day you could see Kitterlund from the marina. It was the last big rocky islet before the open sea, about thirty miles from the Kipneash headland. The people of Kipneash said that Mother Nature had kicked the tip of the isle off into the sea as a home for the birds and seals, where the humans would not bother them.

'Mam promised to swim out there with me, before...' Percy began, but the words melted away as he recalled the state his mother was in.

'The fishing boats never go west of Kitterlund. Have you never noticed? They all go east.'

Marnie was right, it was something Goldie had talked about when he was teaching Percy and Nell how to captain the *Mab*.

Marnie stared at her bony, wrinkled hands. As she raised her head she wiped a tear from her cheek with the ball of her hand. 'I have said too much. Your poor mother. She has enough to worry about. But it is so important that you, Percy Shearwater, know the facts, in case you start to feel *the pull*. I had to warn you. Let's leave it at that. No more of this! I don't want your mother bothered by this concern.'

'Is she going to die?' asked Percy.

'No. She must leave Port Kipneash. If she agrees to do that, she has hope.' Marnie's eyes lacked the surety they usually held. Regardless of their grandma's half-hearted reassurances, Percy and Nell both knew that they were already losing their mam.

'Hope isn't enough. I want it to be certain. I want to know she will be OK. Hope is nothing,' growled Percy. 'And what about me? Will it happen to me too? Will I fade away, like my mam?'

There was silence in the cabin. Fear wasn't an emotion that Percy Shearwater was used to feeling, but it was there, burning inside his stomach. With the fear grew frustration which knotted in his throat and rushed into his chest. His face turned red, his eyebrows knitted themselves in the middle, his eyes shrank while his pupils engorged to deep black swells.

Marnie took hold of Percy's hands and looked into the depths of his eyes. 'Listen to me, my boy. You will have a marvellous life. And, one day, you will move away from here and you will find balance.'

'What if I don't want to move away? What if I want to stay here, in Port Kipneash, like Mam does?'

'That is a decision you will need to make. But you will have to find a *balance*. You will have to search it out. It won't be easy. You will understand it one day.' Marnie smiled and gently stroked Percy's cold hand. 'You remind me so much of Fynlo, Percy. He was so very strong. But even he could not fight *the pull*.' Marnie reached for Percy's neck and let her bony, gold-adorned fingers glide over Percy's delicate pink gills. 'Oh, I have said too much.'

Marnie leapt from her seat and ran to the deck of the *Queen Mab*, bashing into the walls of the cabin as she did, tripping over her long coat. The children followed, confused.

Marnie and the twins stood on the deck of the *Queen Mab*. Marnie held on to the metal balustrade that ran around the edge of the boat. She opened up her arms and looked to the sky. Nell and Percy looked up too. A huge swell of birds swarmed and made beautiful swirls in the dusky sky. They were starlings circling in waves, synchronised like parts of a huge body. A murmuration like none any of them had ever seen before.

The birds circled lower and Marnie repeated, this time in a whisper, 'You can feel my anguish, can't you? I know, I know. I have said too much.' She looked at the children, tears running down her face. 'Your grandfather is of the sea, but I am of the sky. A great, mysterious force lives within our family. Push it down, push it away. Fight it and live a normal life.'

The sound of Percy's voice was hidden by the rumble of the sea and the wind and the birds, but if Nell had tried hard enough, she might have heard him whisper, 'It starts in Kitterlund.'

Chapter 13

Connor Price's House

CONNOR

'I can't believe you've never heard *gillic*,' said Percy.

'It's not a real thing. Seriously, it's made up.' Connor laughed.

'Mam can do it, it's like... *ieeek, coooo, eeeik!*' squeaked Percy. 'I mean, it's a bit old fashioned I guess, it's old-school gilly. Ask your dad.'

Connor was in stitches, unable to breathe for laughing so much, holding his tummy with his hands. 'Fine, fine, I submit! Stop it, it hurts!'

Percy threw a cushion at his friend. Connor could see that Percy was trying to smile, but he was distracted.

The boys were still cold from being in the sea too long that night. They'd created a few codes using nods and hand gestures; neither boy had learned to use sound under the water yet. There was so much they still had to learn about being gilly. Connor couldn't imagine making a sound that could be heard in the water.

Percy had insisted on practising his sea-bed walking and his lights-off swimming; he was different today, determined. Connor watched his friend carefully, quietly warming up by the gas fire. Twitching away at the dinner table.

Dinner was being served; they always had fish when Percy came over. Tonight it was fish and chips, and it was a celebration – Jonah was home.

'Do you like the haddock, Percy?' asked Janie eventually, not used to Percy being so quiet.

'Yes, thank you.' Percy smiled. 'My dad says you should always have haddock at the chippy, it's the best,' he replied.

Percy wolfed his food down silently, then politely asked for more.

'Whoa there, tiger! You'll get indigestion!' smiled Jonah.

'Sorry Mr Price, I get...'

'We know, really hungry when you've been swimming.' Mrs Price smiled and shook her head. 'So, did you find any treasure tonight?'

'*Mum...*' Connor said, rolling his eyes.

'Sorry love.' She grinned as she cleared the plates away.

'How's your mum, Percy? We haven't seen her on the *Monabeg* for some time now,' asked Jonah.

'Not good. She's really poorly. I'm going to help her. I'm going to save her,' Percy said with a seriousness that invited Connor to search his friend's face for answers. Something was not right with Percy today, that was for sure.

'Good for you, Percy. I'm sure she'd be very happy to know that you are looking out for her. I've had terrible spells, and you know our poor Connor... well. It can happen to us all. Us gillies.' Mr Price gave a silent sigh and he looked out of the window; you could see the sea from Connor's house. 'It's nice to finally meet you, Percy, I'm glad Connor has someone he can swim with when I'm away.'

Connor watched his mother's face turn a shade paler with this talk of the sea. She still worried too much.

'You know Connor has had some difficulties... with his condition.' Connor blushed and stroked his left gill, his weakness, as his father spoke. 'But I must say, Connor, you have amazed me with how strong you are growing, and I am sure that it is partly down to *you*, Percy. You are a good friend.'

Connor watched his father as he paused, lost in a thought, somehow sadder than before.

'My work has kept me away so much.' Jonah shook his head. This was a conversation they'd had before, many times. 'Our seas are in crisis, now more than ever. My work becomes more demanding by the day.'

'How long are you going to be working on the *Monabeg* for, Mr Price?' asked Percy.

'I don't know yet. Maybe a year. Maybe more. We'll see.'

'And then will you go back to Limiona?'

'We'll see. I suppose we'll have to,' said Jonah. 'To maintain our balance.'

'But I'm stronger now – now I have Percy to swim with. I'm stronger *here*,' said Connor, with more than a little bit of desperation in his voice. Jonah was a man of science, and Connor could see that his father wasn't going to fall for any suggestion that it was Kipneash, with its cold waters and long winters, that had gifted Connor his extraordinary recovery. *He must know*, Connor thought to himself, as a cold rush of memory filled his bones like the cold rush of water he felt at the start of every one of those secret night-time swims.

A knot rose in Connor's stomach at the thought of leaving Kipneash. It felt like home. He caught his mother's eye and he wondered whether she felt the same way.

* * *

'Go on, then,' said Connor when he and Percy were alone.

'What?' Percy whispered back.

'You've been strange all day. And now this stuff about saving your mum. What are you up to, Percy? You're planning something, aren't you?' Connor could feel the twinkle in his own eye.

'OK, I'm not supposed to tell you, but... listen...'

Connor's eyes widened as his friend divulged all he knew. If there was an adventure to be had, he wasn't going to be left behind. Not again. Connor Price was owed an adventure or two.

Chapter 14

Everything is Not Normal

PERCY

Percy Shearwater always picked the hardest trees to climb. Once, Goldie had to call the fire brigade to pluck his son free from a branch ten metres in the air. He had got stuck at three metres, but instead of finding a safe way down, he climbed higher so that he could cross to the next tree which looked easier to descend. He got stuck there, and climbed even higher still. It was a wildly ambitious plan, and if he had been a grown man it might have worked. But he lacked the strength to carry his own weight when hanging from the branch – a key part of his strategy. No, Percy was not known for his forethought and planning. He was not afraid of risk.

Perhaps it was a measure of just how scared Percy was that, with the help of Connor, and with almost military precision, he was compiling an exhaustive list of all the potential risks that he may encounter, should Doona ever beckon him. Should he be too weak to resist *the pull*. He called it 'Operation Preparation'.

'Here,' whispered Connor as he sat in a quiet corner of Port Kipneash library, pointing to a page in *An Almanac of Sea Adventures*. 'It says that fish have something called a "swim bladder", it helps them change their dive—'

'You didn't know about the swim bladder? You've got one too,' Percy interrupted, shaking his head in bewilderment at his friend's ignorance.

'Have I?' said Connor, poking at his belly. 'What about this: if a diver spends too long deep underwater and then comes back up too quick, he can get bubbles in his blood and it can—'

'Yes, Connor, the bends. I know.' Percy was trying not to lose patience, it wasn't like him to be easily irritated, that was Nell's speciality. But, unlike Connor, Percy wasn't excited by the awe and wonder of this fact-finding mission. He was logging information like it was ammunition.

'They call it decompression sickness here.' Connor paused, his eyes widening. 'Can gillies get the bends?'

'Yes they can. Uh,' groaned Percy. 'That's another one to add to the list.' He felt deflated as he scribbled in his notepad.

The library was the biggest building in Port Kipneash. It was one of the oldest too. People travelled from all over the world to see its marine biology and maritime collection. With so many nooks and crannies, the library felt like a deep underwater cave of silence and serenity. It was lit by hundreds of small brass lamps and the tall rows of shelves went on for what seemed like miles and miles. The intricate wood carvings of sea creatures on the ceilings and pillars scared Percy if he looked at them too hard. They were both mythical and maniacal.

Everything in the library was brown, wooden and dark – except for the green leather table tops, which were full of scratches and scuffs from cradling battered books and being leant on for learning. Like Goldie's clocks, they retained the scars of the past. Only, this time, the scars were left by old ideas rather than ancient repairs.

'What are you two looking at, eh?' Nell's voice punctuated the silence like a thorn. Percy threw his arms over the paper in front of him as his sister appeared, arms folded, back straight, glaring down her nose at the boys.

'Just some research,' he said quickly.

'Likely story.' She squinted at him, as if trying to read his thoughts. 'I hope you're not up to anything, Percy Shearwater.'

'It's not really any of your business, though, is it Nell?' grunted Connor.

Percy watched his sister's eyes widen as she looked at his friend. A harshness had begun to grow between his sister and his friend. He knew that for Nell, the brittle atmosphere between them was envy. She'd always been jealous of gillies, and it was inevitable that she would feel left out. All Connor wanted to do was be a gilly with Percy, and Nell's involvement was just interference.

'We aren't up to anything, Nell,' smiled Percy. 'Just... reading. What are you doing?'

'I'm researching Archibald Knox, like you two should be, for Mrs Angkor. Did you forget that's your homework, not' – she grabbed the book that was lying on the desk in front of Percy – '*Great Gilly Explorers*.'

'Nell! It's here!' A shout disguised as a whisper came from behind a bookcase on the other side of the library. Nell shook her head at Percy before turning and following the voice.

'She likes to stick her nose in, doesn't she, your sister?,' groaned Connor as he turned another page.

'She's OK. She just feels a bit left out.'

'If she's that bothered about it she could just put on her scuba gear and come swimming with us. But she never does. I know she thinks I get in the way.'

Connor was right. Nell did think he got in the way. But it wasn't as simple as that. Percy was keen to change the subject.

'You know, Connor, if I ever do go to Doona, I'll have to go it alone,' Percy whispered. 'I appreciate your help, I really, really do. But I couldn't put you at risk too.'

Connor said nothing, he kept flipping over the huge pages of the almanac.

'Like last night... It scared me,' said Percy seriously.

'That shark? It scared me too...' said Connor.

'No, Connor. It scared me how scared *you* were. You just disappeared. I was out for ages looking for you. I thought you'd been hurt, or something.'

106

'I'm sorry. It took me by surprise. It was a *shark*, Percy! And... I suppose I panicked... and I... I was ashamed of being so scared ... So I just went home.'

'Shhhhhh! No talking in the library!' A loud, shrill voice came from the front desk.

Percy continued softly, his back hunched towards the desk, as if making himself appear smaller might make his voice quieter. 'Yes, but it was a *basking* shark. They aren't dangerous, Connor.'

The basking shark was a massive beast, and with its huge open jaws, it looked like a dangerous predator, but it would never have touched them. The Jetty Beach basking shark was well known to the Shearwaters. It would disappear for months at a time, but it always came back. Glimpsing the basking shark was a joy, a privilege, a sign of the fruitful harvest of the home waters.

The boys sat in silence. Percy, who never felt comfortable in any kind of argument, could feel the tension growing between him and Connor. He watched as his friend's pale complexion flushed, and he considered whether he had been right to embarrass him by mentioning the previous night.

'You can finish the research yourself.' Connor's voice was small but undeniably filled with fury. 'I guess I'm not quite gilly enough to understand it all, anyway.' Connor shoved the book across the desk to Percy and stormed out of the library.

Percy instantly felt bad. Connor had been helping him. He'd even come up with the idea of buying pouches of baby food to take to Doona. *Baby food is perfect. It's small, doesn't need to be kept in the fridge. It's airtight, so it won't go bad in the water. You'll thank me later*, he'd said. It was good thinking.

But Connor Price did not only have good ideas. He had big and dangerous ideas too. If only Percy had seen the signs.

Chapter 15

Bad News

PERCY

Percy was sat with Goldie and Nell in front of the fire, the TV gently humming as Marnie fussed in the kitchen, talking to herself and moving things around, fretting over something that no one had the energy to ask her about.

It was stormy outside. The rain hammered sideways and the wild wind had no direction at all. The walk home from school had been miserable, especially because things were still not quite right again between him and Connor.

Nell opened her sketch-book and Goldie peered over her shoulder. 'Is that the *Mab*?' he asked, pointing to a small boat in the middle of an angry, tempestuous sea.

She nodded.

Dina limped down the stairs and sat on the sofa, next to Goldie. She silently reached for the remote control and turned off the TV. Nobody complained. There was a heavy feeling in the air.

While Marnie stood behind the sofa, hands tucked in her lacy, pearl-trimmed apron, the Shearwater children sat at their mother's feet. Percy let the heat of the fire warm his cheeks. He turned each side of his face towards the fire, evening out the warming caress.

Goldie began to speak.

'We are fast approaching winter. Your mother needs to be in a warmer place. Warmer air. Warmer sea.'

'We aren't moving, are we? Not *now*,' asked Percy with desperation. Doona was a dream he had allowed himself to bathe in. He wasn't ready to let that dream fade away. *The pull* was taking its hold.

'No, well, yes, I mean...'

'What your father is trying to say is that *we* need to go away, until I have my strength back,' said Dina softly. Reaching out for Goldie's hand, she made it clear that by 'we' she meant the two of them, not the twins. 'We haven't taken this decision lightly – the last thing on this earth that I want to do is miss a single day with you, you know that don't you?' A tear ran down Dina's pale face. 'But, I don't want you to miss school, I don't want to uproot you, I don't want to drag you away from your home. And the truth is, we don't know how long we will need to be away. If I can get myself right over the winter, if I don't let things get any worse, we can enjoy a wonderful spring and summer together. It's just... The winter... I don't think I can...'

'Mam... could you... might you... maybe... *die*?' Nell sniffed as she reached over to touch Dina, clinging on to her trouser leg like she did when she was little. 'It's that serious, isn't it?'

'Yes, Nelly, darling. It is. I could die.'

'We should all go,' Nell said. 'I'll pack my bags and leave right now. I know you don't want to move us, I understand that. But I don't care. We should all move to the Indian Ocean. You'll be safer there.'

'Maybe. But it's not guaranteed. Gillies can never really be sure how they will find balance. And, besides, I cannot leave Port Kipneash.' Dina looked down at her hands. They had become a mess of veins and bones, a criss-cross of knotted twine. 'This is temporary. Your father and I will be going to the Indian Ocean, to stay with my cousin Ailish, and we will return when I am better.'

'And what about if you get weak again? If not next year, then the year after? What then?' asked Percy.

'Then we will go back. We will go as often as we have to.' Goldie gently rubbed Dina's back and gave a weak smile.

Nell shook her head. She was trying to hide her frustration, but Percy could see that it simmered barely beneath the surface, rising in her cheeks. 'Let's just move! Let's all go, forever, I don't care!'

'Well, I do! We will not leave Kipneash!' growled Dina, coughing as she shouted, the words taking their toll on her weak and wilting frame. 'I have a job to do here. And regardless of that, this is your home.'

'This will pass. When we return, your mam will be strong again—' began Goldie.

'But what if it doesn't work?' Percy interrupted. 'You've said yourself that it's not guaranteed. This might not be the answer. What then?' Sadness inflamed his whole body, and there was another feeling too. *The pull*, he thought. It was growing, building, getting stronger with every tear he held back.

'We will have to see.' Dina said, softly.

'Grannie Marnie will take care of you, and her friend Otto will be coming to help.' Goldie smiled. 'You'll be in safe hands. The time will fly by. We'll be back before you know it.'

'You'll be away for our birthday on Christmas Eve,' whispered Nell as a tear ran down her face. Nell's shoulders shook as Dina reached out to her and held her close.

Memories of past Christmas Eves spent celebrating their birthday floated through Percy's mind like the delicate shells that peppered Jetty Beach. But they crumbled to dust at the sound of Nell's sobs.

'Don't go, I can make it better, I can, I promise!' shouted Percy. He could feel Nell's eyes burning into him.

Everyone was silent.

'What if....' whispered Dina, 'what if we say that, instead of leaving you here, we are just going on a holiday?' Dina wiped a tear from her cheek. 'What if we say that, if I am well enough, we will return for Christmas?'

'Do you promise?' asked Nell, brushing away her own tears with the cuff of her sleeve as yet more tears took their place.

She was met with a thunderous silence, as their parents nodded unconvincingly. Percy knew that a soundless, swirling storm would be brewing in his sister's heart; that it would be rising, until she thought she was alone. She would go out into the woods and scream until it hurt. He had seen her do it before.

'Well, that's settled!' announced Marnie. 'Right! Homemade cod fishcakes on a bed of fresh salad with samphire and a warming udon broth to start.' Marnie pirouetted on the spot and skipped off to the kitchen with a bounce that was entirely inappropriate for the mood in the room.

Nell and Percy followed while Mam curled up for a nap and Goldie stared into the flames. The hum of the TV resumed. The twins found their grandmother hiding in the larder sniffing, wiping her wet cheeks and pretending to look for gravy.

'I don't think you'll need gravy tonight, not with broth,' said Nell. Percy watched his sister attempt a smile.

'Oh, what am I like? *Soy loca!* Of course we don't need gravy tonight. I must be losing my mind.'

Percy handed her a piece of kitchen roll. 'Dry your eyes, Marnie.'

'Don't you leave me too, Percy Shearwater,' Nell muttered, just loud enough for Percy to hear, as she walked up the stairs to her room.

Chapter 16

Otto

PERCY

The news was still floating in the air like a tattered autumn leaf, clinging to its last shreds of life, when Otto arrived on the Shearwaters' doorstep.

'Hooby-dooby! I've got the right house, then?' Otto was a small man with white hair, a sailor's cap and a pot belly. He had a clean-shaven chin and a white moustache that was so long it hid his lips when he spoke. Percy immediately admired Otto's bold decision to wear shorts despite the bitterly cold mid-November weather. He held a staff, polished and full of knots and small carvings, taller than he was, which made him look like an odd sort of shepherd with no sheep. And no long trousers.

'Ah, Otto is it? I would have picked you up,' said Goldie, startled.

'No need for that, my boy! No need at all, it's no great shakes, is it? You know me, I like a good jog, I does.' Goldie grinned and welcomed Otto in.

'Come in, come in! You must be freezing, can I get you a cup of tea, coffee...?'

'It's not cold out there my boy, not yet, you wait another sixteen hours, yessir, that's when the real wind-chill will start. It'll be blowing a *hoolie*! That said, I would love a cup of hot chocolate my boy, and don't skimp on the chocolate— Wait a minute! Is that, can it be... is that...?' He was pretending not to recognise Marnie, who was pretending to hide behind a coat stand which stood in the corner of the room. She jumped out and ran over and gave Otto a big kiss on his cheek. 'Well, I never! Marnie, me old doll, you look just the same. I has always liked the cut of your jib, have I not, eh? Ah, me old mucker!'

'Oh Otto, of course! You're so *silly* sometimes! *Ridiculo! Absurdo!* It's been three weeks since I saw you last, of course I haven't changed a bit! But you, my darrrrling, where has your beard gone?'

'I couldn't keep that old thing, it'd scare the little ones off! Nope, got rid of that when I got your call, I did. Got my smarts on now. Took a couple of days to look around loose ends. Then I thoughts, *I gotta get to Marnie in a brace of shakes, that old bird needs me and needs-is-musts!*'

Sat on the stairs, Nell leant down to Percy. 'What do you think?' she whispered.

'He's made Marnie go all pathetic.'

Marnie giggled and jumped daintily on the spot while Percy rolled his eyes and rubbed his head.

'And who are these two?' They'd been spotted by Otto. The twins stood up and walked slowly down the last few stairs. 'You must be Nell, and this must be Percy.' Otto smiled kindly.

'That's right. Hello,' said Nell as she offered her hand.

Otto took off his cap and stuffed it into his coat pocket. He licked his hand before wiping smooth his wispy white hair, and then used the same damp hand to shake Nell's.

'Go on, Percy,' called Goldie from the kitchen while Nell surreptitiously wiped her hand on the back of her jeans. Percy complied, hoping that he would be spared the spittle.

'It is an *honour*, sir, an *honour*, to meet you,' said Otto, bowing his head reverentially. 'I has heard all about you from Marnie, I has. I is a man of the sea myself, although I don't have your gift, I has worked with many *courageous* gillies,' he exclaimed, punching the air above his head, 'just like you my lad. The bravest men around.'

Otto had a strange way of talking, and was giddy like a child. But he had kind eyes and Percy liked him.

'I is on me beam ends, I is. Could do with a nice warm choccy, if it's not too presumptuous of me to ask.'

'It's on its way, Otto.' Goldie smiled, already warming the milk at the hob.

'Otto, do make yourself at home,' Dina said, but Otto's attention had turned back to Percy.

'Yes, I'll learn a great deal from a courageous gilly like you, Percy my lad.'

Percy smiled.

'Wait 'til you know him a bit better perhaps, Otto?' Nell grinned as she prodded Percy.

Perhaps it was because everyone was laughing at Nell's joke, perhaps it was the sound of Goldie cursing the milk that had boiled over in the pan, or perhaps it was the noise of the kettle whistling its shrill alarm from the hob, but no one in the Shearwater home seemed to hear as Percy calmly said, 'Oh, I'm courageous all right. Just you wait.'

Chapter 17

Goodbyes

NELL

The day came. Goldie and Dina moved slowly, in no rush. Otto's busy presence in the house had lifted everyone's spirits, apart from Nell's. Her soul was just too heavy. There was no escaping the fact that Otto and Marnie, as interesting as they might be, were only in her home because of Mam's illness. Her poor, poor mam.

'Right, well, this is us, we're ready,' Goldie said as he stood by the front door, bags packed into the boot of the car, coats and shoes on, set to leave.

'Yes,' said Dina, 'all ready.' She gestured for Nell to come to her. 'I'm sorry, darling. I'm sorry I'm not strong enough. Look after Percy, won't you?' she whispered, holding Nell as tightly as her fragile arms could.

Nell closed her eyes and breathed in her mother's sweet smell once more. A handful of Dina's hair came out in her hand as she stroked it, and Nell let go of a tear.

'It's OK, darling. I'll come back stronger. I'll be me again. I promise.' Dina smiled and wiped Nell's tears away with her cold, bony hand.

Nell wanted to tell her mother that she and Percy knew all about Doona. She wanted to confide in her mother how worried she was that Percy might do something stupid.

But she didn't say a word.

There was no use in adding to her poor mother's burden.

Nell stood back and watched as Percy gave Mam and Goldie a tight and silent embrace.

And, through a veil of tears, the children watched as their parents drove away.

Chapter 18

The Diving Pack

CONNOR

'I'm going. I can feel *the pull* and I'm going. I want to go quick, so I can be back before Christmas, when Mam will be home and I can save her.'

Percy was breathless. The words he spoke made his enterprise sound simple, logical. But Connor was not so certain.

'You're going?' said Connor with wide eyes. 'How soon?'

Connor knew this was coming. That day in the library had long been forgiven, but Connor could not forget the way Percy had made him feel: like he wasn't gilly enough, like he wasn't brave enough. Since the day in the library Connor had noticed that Percy was a little more quiet, and a little less willing to share his plans. But Connor knew his friend, and he knew that there was only one thing on Percy's mind: Doona.

Although he knew that Percy was determined to go, Connor couldn't help feeling that it was still too soon. It felt too unreal, sat in Connor's bedroom, with the distant sound of Janie pottering about downstairs. It was nearly time for dinner.

Percy sat on the edge of Connor's bed and bounced his knee up and down like a drill on a building site as he chewed at his fingernail.

'I'm going to the jetty at five. I need you to get a message to Nell, just before seven, that's when she would usually come in to wake me up. It'd take them an hour at least to get ready with the *Mab* and everything, so that would give me three hours to make enough progress that they won't be able to come after me. OK? You have to tell Nell not to follow me, tell her about how ready I am, and that I'll be OK. That I'll be back before Christmas,' said Percy and his voice shook a little. 'I'll be OK.'

'I don't think you're ready, Percy.'

'What do you mean? I know I'm ready. I'm going tomorrow.'

'But your mam – she'll come back stronger, she's going to be OK.'

'How do you know that? How does anyone know? What if she has to leave again?' Percy shook his head. 'I can feel it. I know I can get there.'

'I don't know, Percy. I think we need more time.'

'Time isn't on my mam's side. And one day it'll be me, sat there by the fire, covered in blankets, skin and bone.'

'It'll be me too. It *was* me,' murmured Connor.

'You're a good friend, and I'm grateful for everything you've done.' Percy smiled and patted his friend on the shoulder. 'You don't need to worry, Connor. I'm telling you, *I'm ready*. Marnie says I'm just like Fynlo, and if he can get there, so can I.'

'I don't think you should do this. I think it's too risky. I... I...' Connor was panicking.

'Connor, it's OK,' smiled Percy.

It wasn't OK. Connor rested a finger on his left gill. It was still rough to touch and stung a little when he stroked it. He remembered the maps of veins on his arms, his paper-thin skin. Skin that he was still self-conscious about. The long sleeves that hid the shame of his weak body. He remembered the feeling, lying in one of Janie's salt baths, picturing the world beneath the water, rich in his imagination but always out of reach. There was no way that Janie would let him out on his own again if Percy went missing. He would have to go back to a life of green juice, salt baths, paddling with Janie, night swimming alone in the grimy harbour.

'Will you bring something back, for me? The elixir, from the tree, to help *me*?' said Connor, almost in a whisper. His pale cheeks flushed as he sat on the edge of his bed, his elbows on his knees, staring at the floor.

'Of course I will, Connor,' said Percy.

'Thanks. And I'll tell Nell,' Connor replied. But he knew that it wouldn't happen. Connor Price would not be there to cover for Percy.

'OK. So, my diving pack is ready. I'll have my head torch on, but I'm taking two more torches, rope, matches, my penknife, bandages, spare batteries and some clothes. I'm going to wear a wet suit – I don't know how my body will react to the deepest waters, so I need to be prepared. Seven foil pouches of baby food, and twelve chocolate protein bars. Oh, and my waterproofing has been checked and double checked. Nothing is getting into my pack.' Percy was talking quickly and with authority, and Connor thought back to when they first met just weeks ago. He was serious and determined; he was barely the same boy.

* * *

After dinner, Janie Price offered to drive Percy home.

'That's OK, Mrs Price. I think I'm going to drop by the harbour, take in the lights. I haven't had a stroll down there for ages.'

'OK, Percy. I'll call Marnie and let her know you're on your way. Do you want to go too, Connor?' she asked.

'I have some things to do. I'll see Percy tomorrow, at school, won't I?'

'Yes,' said Percy. The lie stung them both.

When Janie was inside and the boys were stood outside Connor's front door, Connor wished his friend good luck. But Percy was distracted. Connor watched him run away towards the harbour. He knew Percy was going there to say goodbye to Kipneash.

Connor went back inside with a heavy heart. To pack his own bag. Percy's empty reassurance about the elixir from Doona was not enough.

Connor had to go there himself.

Chapter 19

The Dive

PERCY

His alarm clock silently flashed its blue light. The room lit up, but Percy needn't have set an alarm. He had not slept.

He did not feel tired. Adrenaline soared through his body.

His brain was telling him to stop, to roll over in his bed and get some sleep. Forget his stupid plan. Instead, he switched his torch on. It was four o'clock. He would be gone earlier than he had told Connor. But that was no problem, it just gave him even more of a head start. He was master of his own plans now.

Next to his clock was a photo of Mam. Long, dark shining hair, a gleaming smile and a face full of light and life. He sat up in his bed, the crisp cold of the morning biting at his limbs as he lifted the warm, heavy duvet off his body.

He'd made a silent promise to her that he surely couldn't break. Could he?

Maybe this was a bad idea.

He pulled on his wet suit and picked up his bag. *It's OK – just because I'm going to the jetty doesn't mean I'm definitely going to leave, does it?* he thought to himself.

Even when he was making his way through the forest and down to Jetty Beach he was still not sure if this was really it, the beginning. There was still time to change his mind. The choice was still his. The cold chill of the late November air hurt his lungs as he ran faster and faster; running away from the decision that rested heavily on his shoulders. He stumbled as he ran, but he did not fall to the floor. His legs wobbled with nerves. His heart beat faster. He spied the light of the sun edging very slowly into the sky; soon it would turn the dead of night into the dusky hues of morning.

Percy stood on the jetty. He breathed in. A big question was ringing around his head. *How will I ever get back?*

His hands were shaking uncontrollably.

He needed Nell. He might be brave in the water, but she always knew how to navigate life. The tricky things like making the right choices. Understanding consequences. That was Nell. None of this was natural for Percy. He closed his eyes. He could see Nell, disapproving.

With his eyes still closed he also saw Mam's future, and then he saw his own. Connor's, too. He saw flashes of white skin, thin like tissue, pale and flaking. He pictured Mam fighting for each breath she took and her gills oozing, thick and yellow. He knew it was time. The questions would have to wait.

Percy opened his eyes wide and looked around. Three hundred and sixty degrees. If things went wrong, this could be the last time he would see his home. He pushed the thought away and locked it behind a door already bulging with *what ifs*. He breathed in the air and put his fingers to his neck, stroking his gills gently, as if to say, '*do your work, keep me safe*'. He tried not to think of Nell any more, but he couldn't banish her from his mind.

Steadying his shaking hands, Percy pulled a notebook and pen from his pack. Connor would pass the message on, but it wasn't enough. She was his twin, and she deserved something more. He searched for words, but they all sounded stupid. In the end, he wrote: *Nell – I will be back by our birthday, I promise.* And he underlined the word 'promise' three times.

He lay the note under a rock at the end of the jetty.

And with that, he dived into the water, gracefully and silently. Unseen by all the world, except one pair of very interested eyes.

Chapter 20

Connor's Big Mistake

CONNOR

Connor was patient. He knew Percy never stuck to a plan, so he had arrived at the jetty early. As soon as Janie was asleep. It was like the old days.

Fighting sleep and dogged against the cold, Connor had waited patiently. When Percy appeared at the edge of the wood and made his way down on to Jetty Beach, Connor had fought the instinct to call out. Instead he watched as his friend readied himself to dive, and then finally disappeared into the water.

Tired bones ignited by adrenaline, Connor ran to the jetty. He gave Percy a one-minute head start, then dived into the freezing cold water.

The speed of his friend could not be underestimated, and Connor hadn't slept. He was exhausted before he even touched the water. As the cold embraced him, Connor's gilly body adjusted, his eyes making the swiftest transition. The view was crystalline. Despite Percy remaining in sight, just, Connor was petrified that he would lose his trail. Percy was always faster than him. Connor's heart beat with a desperate cadence. Maybe the adrenaline would make his body move faster than it had ever moved before. He hoped so.

Connor could see Percy's feet darting into the distance, a mesh of bubbles swirling behind him. Percy was wearing a head torch but Connor had left his off, not wanting to be rumbled. He would cling to Percy's light.

Connor was glad he had brought his wet suit. He had nagged his mum for one every day since he devised his plan to follow Percy to Doona. It was close, but eventually she gave in, and it was just as well. It was going to get a lot colder, the deeper they went.

He didn't have time to be scared about the deep.

Percy was swimming straight ahead, never slowing down. Never looking back. In minutes, they passed by the wrecked boat. The speed that Percy was going must have disturbed the sea life because a small following of creatures began to join Percy's pilgrimage across the water. First was the leatherback turtle. *Percy will be glad to see him*, thought Connor. Then there were two dolphins that joined the trail, sometimes darting up and out of the water, only to return to the fold. A shoal of herrings were interested for a short time but were soon distracted by some seals who were taking a little bit too much interest in them.

Connor's mind was clear. He listened only to his own breathing, the low *whoosh* of the water through his gills mixed with the gentle hum of lungs on standby, acting in their secondary capacity of supporting the gills. His body felt like a machine; it was working twice as hard as it had ever done before. Electric jolts shot down his legs, battling with the fatigue. Still, he laboured on.

They were now beyond the Port Kipneash headland, it was as far as Connor had ever swum before. His knees started to buckle when he flicked his feet. His body was becoming tired and he couldn't hold his swimming posture. It started to feel like he was swimming through syrup. Not for the first time in his life, he felt more human than gilly. His left gill throbbed and stung, and he cursed himself for ever believing that he would be able to keep up with Percy. He let his body stop and float gently; he rested.

Just as Connor Price was readying himself to give up, he felt a nudge. A prod to his back. It was gentle at first, but it shunted him forward with the force of a fist when he failed to turn around.

Shocked and confused, Connor twisted his body round to see what was behind him. Two gleeful, shining black eyes stared back at him. A long rubbery beak opened, revealing a toothy grin: there, right next to him, was a dolphin. They were eye to eye in the stillness of the sea. Connor was unnerved, unsure of what to make of his aquatic stalker. Could this be aggression? It didn't seem so. He shook his head at the dolphin. He tried to slowly rise to the surface, but the dolphin nudged him again.

He followed the dolphin's silent command and took hold of its fin. Connor gripped the rubbery skin of the dolphin, his fingers and knuckles white with the effort. As water pushed past his body, he felt like he was being jettisoned through soft floating clouds, weightless. Connor smiled. He wondered if these dolphins might be allies, fellow night swimmers who knew him of old, who knew what he had been through.

When he could see Percy's torchlight he let go of the fin, not ready to face his friend yet. And as the sun hinted at its glow in the sky above, he knew that soon the sea would be warmer, and day would break.

Chapter 21

Nell Raises the Alarm

NELL

Nell tripped on a root as she lost her footing. She hit the ground. With leaves in her hair and mud in her mouth she scrambled back up and sped on.

The previous night she had filled several pages of her sketch-book with pictures of a rocky islet cave in the middle of the open sea. Inside, it was lit by a shard of light. There were paintings all over the walls, shadows that she could barely make out. It was a place full of bad omens and death.

As soon as Nell awoke in the morning, she opened her sketch-book to look again at what she had drawn. It had haunted her dreams. She knew immediately that Percy was gone. There was no need to check his bed. It would be empty.

She didn't stop to get dressed or put shoes on. She was wearing her bed socks and a nightie, and had dragged a coat behind her, too distracted to put it on. The cold November morning was chilling her to the bone, but still she ran. Her socks were so clogged with soggy mud that they flapped round her ankles and the stones and twigs of the forest bed were irritating her feet; they would itch from tiny scratches by the time she returned home.

Her eyes were still sleep-sore, heavy and half-open. Once she had reached the edge of the long grass, run across the sand and stopped dead at the end of the jetty, she rubbed them so that they would focus.

But the bay was deserted.

The wooden slats of the jetty felt warm from her brother's presence. Maybe it was a twin thing; maybe she imagined it. When she saw the note, she realised it had been placed there some time ago. Maybe hours. The jetty was no longer frost-dry with the frozen winter ice. The slowly rising sun had melted away the ice, and with it Percy's ink. A series of big blue tide-marks were left behind. She could see every word, but through a strange shadow, as if it didn't want to be read – like the strokes of the pen had run away. Just like her brother had run away from her. Just like she wanted to run after him now.

She scoured the horizon for signs of life. The sea was big, and calm. It looked empty and dead, but she knew there was life beneath. She hobbled back to the house.

'Where have you been? Where is Percy?' said Marnie, covering Nell with a blanket and gasping as she saw Nell's feet, bright pink with the cold, her soggy bed socks now discarded. 'Nell? My love? Speak to me, dear. You're worrying me. Otto is out looking for you.'

'He's gone.'

'Yes, *ma cherie*, he has gone looking for you and your brother,' said Marnie as she walked back to the table and stirred a cup of cocoa.

'No. Not Otto. Percy. *Percy* has gone.'

'Where? Where has Percy gone?'

Nell opened her hand. She took the delicately folded note and laid it out on the table. Marnie picked it up and took it to the window where the light shone through it.

'*You* know where he's going, don't you,' said Marnie, resigned.

Nell stared at the flames as they licked the windows of the fire, threatening to burst out and consume them all. 'He's going to Doona, Marnie. He's on his way. But he's in danger. I drew a cave. I don't know why, but I think it's an omen, I think...'

Marnie sat down next to Nell at the kitchen table. 'Is your heart telling you to follow?'

'Yes, but I have no idea how... I'm not a gilly. I'll never feel *the pull*.'

'But you know your brother. Get your sketch-book.'

Nell looked at Marnie quizzically.

'Get it, *now*!' Marnie shouted urgently.

'Why are you shouting at me?' whimpered Nell.

'Nell. Get your book, please, *cherie*, it's important.'

Nell's bones shuddered as she walked past Percy's room. His bed was made and his curtains were open. For a moment, she allowed herself to hope that he'd come back. She searched his bed but there was nothing there, so she lay on his floor and looked under it. There was something... Squished between two boxes full of toys that he had outgrown but Nell knew he couldn't bring himself to give away, was an exercise book.

On the cover were the words 'Operation Preparation'. She opened it cautiously, scared of what it would confirm.

'Oh Percy,' she whispered as she turned each page and fought back a rush of fear and frustration. 'Why didn't you tell me?'

'What are you doing Nell?' Marnie called upstairs. She rolled the book into to a tube and put it into her dressing-gown pocket as she ran into her room and grabbed her sketch book.

Back in the kitchen, she lay her sketch-book flat on the table, next to the note.

There was a big bowl of warm salt water under the table. 'Put your feet in there, *chica*,' Marnie said.

The water stung as Nell lowered her feet into the bowl, but it soon began to soothe them and then the itch of healing began.

Marnie whisked her way through the sketch-book. Page after page of seascapes and birds, the *Queen Mab* in the open sea with no shoreline in sight. And then, from just two days ago, a drawing of a man's face, dark pencil and jagged shading, half-hidden. His eyes were squinted and his mouth was curled into a warm and friendly smile.

'It's your grandfather! Do you know what this means?' asked Marnie.

'No. I must have seen a picture of him... I don't know. Why?'

Before Marnie could answer her grandchild's question, Otto burst through the door. 'No sign— Ah, she's back! What a relief! We've been worried about...' Reading their faces, Otto stopped. 'No boy, then?'

Marnie shook her head.

'I found this in his room.' Nell placed the exercise book on the table next to the sketch-book and the note. 'The writing in the book is like a plan, I think. It's Percy's, but I think Connor has written in it too.'

'Oh, it just gets worse.' Marnie shook her head.

'So he's gone. And do we think it's *you know what*?' asked Otto, being careful with his words.

'*The pull.* Yes,' Marnie nodded.

'That boy has bravery on his side, that's for certain. But stupidity too, if you don't mind me saying so, young Nell. Monumental stupidity.' Otto twisted his cap violently in his hands as he paced the room.

'He knows so little, Otto,' said Marnie with a tear in her eye. 'That boy knows nothing of what awaits him.'

Otto shook his head.

'Heed your pictures carefully, take nothing for granted,' counselled Marnie as she took Nell's cold hand in hers. 'You won't feel *the pull*, but you will feel Percy.'

'My pictures. They're premonitions, aren't they?'

'I think so.'

'But, how...?' Nell didn't know what to ask, or even if Marnie would have the answers.

'I don't know. I told you before, your grandfather is of the sea and I am of the sky. I feel a connection to the winds, the tides, the birds. And they feel a connection to me. Call it magnetism, call it what you like. But one thing is a complete unknown to me, to any of us...'

'And what's that?'

'Although the sea and the sky combined in your grandfather and I, Dina simply inherited the sea, the gills, nothing more. But in *you*, I see something else. I believe your pictures are the consequence of your strange and wonderful genetics. The power of us all, combined.' Marnie looked deep into Nell's eyes. 'I believe that your pictures are premonitions, and that one day you will be able to command them at your will. Because of your unique inheritance, you have an extraordinary insight into the world: the mysteries of the sea and sky are combined in you. Your pictures may be something of a mystery to us all *now*, but I doubt that will remain the case for very long.' Marnie smiled and stroked Nell's hair away from her face.

Otto scurried to the window. 'The sand martins, they're there,' he said, craning his neck to look to the sky.

'Between us, we can do this. We have Otto, he is not to be underestimated. And I will play my part,' said Marnie.

'I'll get the *Mab* fuelled up,' said Otto, jumping to action. 'And get the supplies.'

Nell nodded, she knew that there was no other option. They were going to Doona.

Chapter 22

Janie Price

NELL

'So, that is what we are doing now, preparing to go after them,' finished Nell as she and Marnie stood in Janie Price's kitchen. Janie was still but her hands were shaking and her skin had turned a deathly shade of pale.

'Otto is the greatest fisherman and sailor there is,' Marnie said. 'He will guide us to Percy and Connor.'

'Connor isn't as strong as Percy in the sea,' said Janie, as she picked up her phone and began to dial. There was a note stuck to the fridge reminding her to pay for Connor's school trip to Kipneash Maritime Museum. Nell shuddered. 'I'll have to call the school, tell them he'll not be in today.'

'We think they may be gone for more than one day, Mrs Price.'

Janie looked shocked. 'What do you mean?'

'Percy left a note to say that he was going to explore...' Nell watched her words carefully, evading the weight of the word 'Doona'. 'The note said that he would be back by...' She paused.

'Please, Nell.'

'... by Christmas.'

Janie sat down at the table and rested her face in her hands. 'We need to call the police. Report them as missing. If only Jonah was here...'

If only Mam had been strong enough. If only Percy had never heard of Doona. If only Nell had been born gilly. There were a lot of *if only*s.

Nell and Marnie stayed with Janie until the police arrived, sitting silently while Janie paced the floor, looked out of the window, shook her head and wiped her damp cheeks. It was just as Nell had silently predicted – the police didn't seem to know what to make of it all. Two gilly runaways off to explore the ocean; gillies doing what gillies do. They made notes, shifted nervously, smiled kindly. But there was nothing to be done. Gillies were a law unto themselves.

As they reached the edge of the town and the rubble road that led home, Nell and Marnie found Otto loading up the car to drive down to the jetty.

Overhead, the starlings were back. They were in murmuration, dark rainclouds swirling in graphite patterns about their heads. They were pushing towards the sea then retreating back above her head. They were moving like the waves of the tide.

'Come on, my girl! You'll see plenty more of that soon!' shouted Otto.

Nell ran to the house, grabbed the few things she needed – her sketch-book, Percy's exercise book, her pencils, scuba gear and wet suit. She tore out a page from her book and scribbled a note for Goldie, just in case, folding it and leaving it on her bed. She wondered if she would ever see her room again, if she would ever see Goldie and Mam again.

She left the house. She did not turn back.

Chapter 23

Connor and Percy Have a Lot to Talk About

PERCY

Percy's arms were like jelly, his legs felt like they belonged to someone else. He allowed himself to float on the surface of the water. Goldie called it 'playing dead'; it filled his father with fear.

Finally mustering enough energy to pull himself from the water on to a rock, he looked around. The sun was low and bright. He had reached the last islet before Kitterlund. He breathed quickly and deeply. The islet was home to a colony of guillemots. Small withered trees had tried to grow, but failed to thrive. He surveyed the jagged surface of the rock. He was on his way, and no one would catch up, not at the rate he had been going. He would be at Kitterlund before lunch-time.

Percy felt a tsunami of courage and pride rush around his body, pumping with the adrenaline in his veins. He screamed a loud primal victory scream at the top of his lungs and punched the air all around him. He closed his eyes, and felt the strength inside that had come from taking this first leap, alone. He allowed a proud smile to spread across his face as he stared into the endless sea ahead of him.

As his eyes opened, his smile vanished. He could hear something. It was the quiet sound of breathing, coming from behind him.

Slowly, he turned round, unsure of what he would find.

Connor Price.

Percy's legs shot out from under his body and he fell back on to the hard, rocky ground. He let out a very not-brave-sounding squeal and rubbed the hand that had broken his fall.

'Connor! What are you doing? You can't... What are you doing here?'

'I'm coming too.'

'No, you are not. How did you... Is the *Mab* here? Did you come with Nell?'

'I'm alone. And I *am* coming with you,' said Connor, sounding defiant but looking quite unsure as he blinked his eyes in a nervous twitch. 'I can either come with you, or go on my own. I'd rather come with you.'

'You can't come with me, you *idiot*. I can't believe this. You're not really here. I'm hallucinating. I'm tired. I need...' Percy pushed by Connor to get to the edge of the rock. He began to lower himself down, to get back into the water and push on to Kitterlund. 'What are you playing at, Connor? This is so *stupid*. You won't make it. You're too weak. You'll stop us both from getting to Doona and then my mum will die! I'll never forgive you for this! What about this do you not understand, Connor? You *cannot* come with me!' Percy's face was bright red, his eyes were wet from tears of anger. But something was stopping him from getting back into the water.

'I *can* do it, Percy. Trust me. I'm... I'm *sick* of people telling me I'm weak. I'm not. I got here, didn't I?' Connor blushed.

'I haven't got time for this, Connor. I don't want to have to explain to your mum that you died out here following *me*. Go back.'

149

'No!'

'Go back, you *idiot!*'

'I won't. Stop calling me an idiot, Percy. This isn't you. You're better than this.'

Percy was furious. If he had been thinking rationally he might have seen there could be benefits to having a companion. But he was blinded by an unfamiliar anger. He stood up and threw himself towards Connor, punching him firmly in the belly. Connor screamed, winded, and lashed out, arms flailing. Both boys hit out viciously at each other, grabbing and pushing at whatever they could. Connor jumped backwards into the water, narrowly missing a huge rock. He began to sink under. But within a few seconds he was back at the surface, lip bleeding, twice as determined.

'This isn't you. This isn't what my friend Percy would do,' he said, wiping the blood from his lip with the sleeve of his wet suit.

'Friends don't lie, Connor. Friends are honest. Do you know how important this is? It's not a game. My mam is going to die! *Actually die!*'

Percy began to sob. He sank down to his haunches.

'Why did you hide it from me, Connor? Why didn't you say anything? Was it because you knew it was a totally *stupid* idea?'

'You're an idiot sometimes, Percy Shearwater,' said Connor as he shook his head and swam back towards his friend. The waves lapped only centimetres from them, and the sun was beating down through the bracing autumn air. 'I'm your *friend*, Percy. You just punched me,' he said. 'It's not like you to do something like that. It'll be good for you to have me around. Hey, Mrs Angkor would say, "team work makes the dream work"...'

'Dream? Is that what you think this is? More like a night-mare,' growled Percy, pulling himself up to his feet. He sighed. His anger was waning.

He looked down to the sea. Out here, he was always going to be on the precipice between safety, and the steep, endless drop into untold dangers. With Connor along for the ride, that precipice was going to be twice as dangerous and Percy was twice as likely to fall from it, never to return. But Connor was his friend.

Percy was sorry, but not sorry enough to say so. 'Fine. Let's get a move on. I *will* leave you behind if you get too slow.'

He turned to take one last look at the rock behind him and the guillemots, idly content in their home. A few feet from where he was stood was the opening to a cave. He took a cautious step forward and peered in. Just below the point at which shadow was cast and darkness began to take over, where none of the cracks and crevices of the rock could be seen, there was a line where light and dark met. Just under that line there was a message daubed in a silvery kind of paint.

My journey began here. Let yours end here.

'Well, that's a stupid message.'

Percy turned to his friend. 'What do you mean?'

'Well, whoever wrote that message either gave up and came back to paint it, or got to Doona and then came back. So it's not exactly going to put us off, is it? A good warning would be a pile of dead bones on the rocks, or a skull on an empty boat. A note? Survivors write notes.'

Percy stared at his friend. Perhaps Connor was wilier than Percy had ever given him credit for.

Chapter 24

The Razorbill

NELL

'I think they're leaving us, Marnie!' shouted Nell as she looked up to the sky. The starlings had been making their hypnotic, winding shapes above their heads since the *Mab* had departed, but they had gone as far as they wanted to for now, and were turning back.

Nell and her grandmother looked up to the sky. 'They'll be back, no fear,' Marnie said.

Nell opened her sketch-book and held her pencil. She couldn't think what to draw. She wanted to talk to Percy, to know he was OK. All she could see when she closed her eyes were the dangers that awaited him. A shark sped towards her with open jaws and she opened her eyes. Was her imagination running away with her, or was this Percy's fate? She couldn't bear to think about it. She closed her book.

Nell couldn't be alone with her thoughts. They were leading her up dark and dangerous alleys. She sidled up to Marnie and rested her head on her grandmother's shoulder. They sat silently together. Nell's eyes closed and she drifted.

When she opened her eyes, Nell found herself looking directly at the razorbill; it was sat on the balustrade of the boat, eerily still. Nell clocked its jet black feathers, its soft baby down. That striking white patch darting under its body. Its thick beak was deep and blunt; it looked like a stately Roman emperor. It wasn't making a sound, and neither was Marnie. They were trance-like, starring at one another. After a few more seconds, Marnie nodded and the bird flew away. Marnie rose silently and took herself below deck.

'Don't worry little lady, your grandmother hasn't lost heart. She's thinking. All this is taking it out of her, but that's a good thing.' Otto smiled kindly as Nell looked over to him for reassurance. 'Nothing that was easy ever worked, and ain't that the truth.'

By the time Marnie reappeared with three cups of mint tea on a small tray, the boat was almost still, bobbing gently as they reached a point parallel to a rocky islet littered with guillemots and petrified trees.

They floated slowly past and Otto called out 'Percy, lad, are you there? We ain't gonna stop you boy! We just wants to know you is safe, is all!' But the empty cave of the islet simply echoed back mockingly.

Otto began to take down the sail. No one said a word, the three of them all looked on, towards the cave. He'd been there. All of them felt it.

'No, Otto, leave it up,' she ordered.

'We should check, see if the lad's left anything there. Could be hiding.'

'Keep going. There's nothing here,' said Nell. She surprised herself with the certainty in her voice. She picked up her sketch-book again. She drew with fury and held her picture up to the light. 'There's another cave.'

Chapter 25

A Game of Trust

CONNOR

'Kitterlund!' cried Connor breathlessly, tugging Percy towards the surface.

Percy emerged. Connor watched him squint and adjust his eyes so that he could focus on the far distance, out of the water.

'It's Kitterlund, it must be! Let's stop for a bit,' said Connor, hopefully.

'We can't afford to.'

'We could stop for a break, ten minutes, just for a cocoa.'

'Nell and Marnie will be following us by now. The weather is on their side today, we may only be an hour or two ahead of the *Mab*. If they catch up with us, they'll make us go back. We won't be safe until we're past the eddies. Come on,' Percy commanded, and the boys continued.

The Kipneash waters were carrying them fast, but not fast enough. The afternoon winds were bracing and the waves were building up strength. The boys dodged currents as they swam, watching for danger signs while ploughing the surf as fast as they could.

Percy led Connor deeper. It was harder to swim, but Connor understood – staying further below the surface of the water might help them escape the surface currents caused by the winds at sea, even if it did mean that the cold would be harsher against their skin, harsher in their gills.

Connor tried not to think about the jellyfish. Killer whales weren't unknown in these waters either, 'Operation Preparation' had taught him *that*. He swam behind Percy, who propelled himself fearlessly through the water. Percy didn't flinch when a fish came into their path, he never changed his course, he never looked back. *Perhaps that's what* the pull *does to you*, thought Connor. His own weak pace was slowing by the mile, but he had a weapon in his armoury.

Percy signalled to Connor that they needed to speak. Out of the sea, their tired heads bobbed.

'Why have we stopped?' Connor panted.

'We can't go this slow, Connor... How did you keep up with me before? I need to know. You're not keeping pace even though I've slowed right down for you. It doesn't make any sense,' shouted Percy above the churn of the sea.

'Fine. The dolphins, they dragged me.'

'What dolphins?'

'You haven't noticed them? Percy, you need to start looking around you. You're going to miss something important if you don't. You're doing this all wrong.'

Percy's head disappeared just under the water. Hovering in the sea by Connor's slowly beating legs were two dolphins and a whole school of porpoises. The dolphins had stuck with Connor.

Percy rose to the surface. 'So?' he spat, wiping his eyes.

'We can tether ourselves to them.'

'What if they lead us the wrong way?'

'You'll know if they send us the wrong way. You can feel *the pull*, right?'

'Can't you?'

Connor shook his head silently.

'Mam would never cut corners like this, it feels wrong.'

'If the dolphins pull us at their speed, it will buy us time to rest on Kitterlund. They could even get us in to the Doona core ring, and there's bound to be an islet where we can rest once we're inside.'

'But...'

'I know you want to disagree with me, Percy, but you know I'm right.'

They tethered themselves to the dolphins using rope which they had hung in loops on the side of their packs. The dolphins were still and made no complaint as Percy and Connor tied the knots tightly enough, but not so tight that they would hurt their new friends. The dolphins made hic-squeak noises that almost sounded like laughing, and Percy finally smiled. Connor looked closely and noticed battle scars across the dolphins' bodies – white marks over skin that had once been all grey.

The dolphins knew the course they were on; they glided through the sea, effortless. The easy tug of the water against Connor's skin was welcome.

It wasn't only the dolphins and porpoises following their route – seals swam by too, gawking with their comical faces at the peculiar duo making their way across the ocean. There was a deep black abyss below the boys' bodies, black and covered in barnacles. It was not the deep-dark-nothing of open water, but a humpback whale. The dolphins changed course briefly to allow the whale to splash magnificently up and out of the sea, seeking out its herring lunch. The sight fed Connor's hope and not his fear. He felt different.

Connor knew the extreme cold of the water. But he also knew the warm comfort of the Foillan Stream, which he had explored alone at night and, more recently, with his friend. The seas of the Follian Stream were not as warm as the Indian Ocean, but they had a special quality only discernible in his gills; they were the temperate, more hospitable waters that had comforted many gillies over the years. Every now and again he would feel the familiar taste of the Follian Stream, its familiar temperature, flowing through his gills. But there was something else too, something equally reassuring and certain that he couldn't at first put his finger on. Eventually, he realised what it was. That sense of conviction and of warmth, like a glow in his belly, was *the pull*.

The pulsing repetition and the slow, churning flow of the open sea comforted Connor as he basked in *the pull*, examining every inch of this new awareness of his surroundings. Eventually, bathed in a soft sort of calm, Connor was rocked into a sleep that he didn't even try to fight, despite the danger of it.

Chapter 26

Kitterlund

NELL

'If our boy has any sense in him, he'll be restin' up here tonight, mark my words,' said Otto optimistically, as he anchored the *Mab* off Kitterlund.

Nell struggled to share Otto's positivity.

They dropped anchor next to a rocky ridge. Kitterlund had no inviting beach; it was a stony punctuation mark in the middle of the wild water. Two other boats were tethered there. They looked much more weather-worn than the *Mab*, with their stench of fish, gaudy patchwork paint, chipped balustrades and smashed-out windows to the cabins; their captains had surely seen some sights.

Nell, Otto and Marnie made their way up the patchy and uneven steps that were cut into the unforgiving rock of the island. Two hundred and fifteen steps up to The Sky, Kitterlund's hostel for seafarers. Nell counted each one. Each one a step closer to Percy. Maybe.

Water had struck Nell as she climbed off the boat. It had soaked one leg of her jeans and the bitter cold was still hitting her like a hammer.

'I think a storm is coming,' Nell called to Marnie as they climbed the last of the steps, wind biting at them, wet hair whipping their faces. The sea was so black below her, it looked like a giant abyss, a bottomless hole. She squinted, tried to see a light shimmering in the distance, the light of a head torch, but there was nothing.

Otto pushed open the heavy door to The Sky and the sound of fiddles lifted out of the bar like smoke rising from the fire at home. A man with three teeth in his mouth and as many strands of hair on his head stood polishing a glass with a scurvy looking rag behind the short wooden bar. Another man sat at a table watching the fiddlers. The music didn't stop but it may as well have done. Big-eyed glances bore into the *Mab*'s crew, as if they were supernatural creatures from the sea.

Otto went to the bar and ordered three cocoas. Nell noticed that the bar man put two overflowing thimbles of an orange syrup from a dusty looking bottle into Otto and Marnie's drinks. Otto didn't complain. The dusty bottle went back in its place behind the bar, on a shelf with a row of other dusty looking bottles.

There were only two tables in The Sky, both directly next to each other, cocooned in a snug of wooden benches. Marnie sat next to the lone man, the solitary customer, as the fiddlers fiddled.

'May we join you?' Marnie said with the biggest smile she could muster, sitting before waiting for a response.

'Aye, you can sweetheart. You from the mainland?'

'Yes, we're following my grandson who is trying to get to Doona. He ran away.'

The man looked up from his glass. He looked directly into Marnie's eyes. 'He's a gilly?'

'Yes, yes he is.'

'Does he have true grit?'

Otto sat down at the table carrying the mugs of cocoa. 'Yes, sir, I does believe it is so.'

'Then don't worry your minds. You go back to your mainland. Your boy will be just fine if he's got *true* grit. Sea-battered, he will be. But you'll see him again someday, I'd wager.'

'What's *true* grit?' asked Nell, settling on a chair, wondering if maybe she had it too.

'Why, little lassie, if you need to ask, then you don't got it.'

Nell frowned. She sipped at her cocoa and listened to the fiddlers play their merry song, but she didn't feel merry. This place was dark, and damp, the cocoa wasn't creamy and the air stank of kippers. The barman told Otto that he was smoking his own fish in the back of the bar. They could try some with a crusty half-loaf of bread if they didn't mind sitting to eat with his other patron. Nell didn't want to eat with him. He smelled of the sea and his hair was all matted and crusty. His beard was tied into a plait and his clothes could have walked out of the bar on their own.

'In my experience, which is as wide as it is deep,' said the stranger, 'two things happen to the brave souls who seek out Doona. They find it and never want to return, or, they are lost to the Dearmad.'

Nell looked up. 'What's the Dearmad?'

'There are them islands, more like rocks, all along the core ring. It ain't too hard to find the Doona core ring, not if you're gilly. And it ain't too hard to navigate them eddies, long as you don't hit a cyclone...' The stranger lifted his hair away from his neck to reveal that half his ear was missing. Nell also noticed his gills – red, crusty and bubbled like Mam's had become. 'Lost my ear and my leg to a cyclone, bashin' and thrashin' around I was, under that water, got too close to the rocks, thought they'd give me shelter. I was wrong, lass. Oh, I was wrong.'

'You're a brave man, sir' said Otto reverentially, sipping his cocoa and wincing at the heat, or maybe at the syrup that the barman had put in his drink.

'No braver than the rest, lad, no braver than the rest.' Otto wasn't a 'lad' by any stretch of the imagination, but Nell nodded to the man nevertheless, willing him to begin again. 'The Dearmad. That *bally* Dearmad. Same pull as Doona, stronger maybe.'

'The Dearmad is a cave, Nell, a cursed cave. It's inside the Doona core ring on the route to Doona, and the legend is—' Marnie began.

166

'No legend, it be *real*,' the man growled.

'Yes, forgive me. The Dearmad is an oubliette,' continued Marnie.

'It steals your memory. Gone. Then it steals your life,' said the man in a low whisper that crackled on the surface. 'I'm no longer a strong man. The cyclone took that from me – there's no swimming for this old gilly, unless my lady-love comes down there with me, holds on to me, else the sea comes for the rest of me. Not satisfied with just one of my legs! It wants the other!' He laughed a curdling, hysterical laugh as he rapped on his wooden leg with his scarred knuckles. The fiddlers stopped for a moment, and the candle on the table, within an inch of death, flickered . 'No, my days of finding Doona are well gone now. I come out here often as I likes, gets closer to those precious waters, keeps me going... just about,' he said, beating his chest with closed fists and grinning a near-toothless grin.

'So, the Dearmad?' said Nell with a gentle nudge in her voice.

'Well, once you gets there, you gots to leave, straight away, every second there takes away what keeps you alive.'

'Is the air that thin inside it?' asked Nell, not understanding the man's riddles.

'No, my little lady. The Dearmad takes away your reasons, your loves – the things you want to live for.'

'Nell, if your brother found himself in that cave, it would wipe clean his memory – he would have no reason to continue to Doona, no reason to return home. If Percy and Connor get stuck in the oubliette, they won't go any further,' explained Marnie.

'But that would be good, wouldn't it? It'd be easy to find them if they just stayed there.'

'Not at all, lady.' Otto grunted and shook his head sternly. 'He'd be trapped, forever. Ain't nobody safe. What, you think you could just go in after him and bring him out? Ain't nothing that easy.'

'The Dearmad is a false friend.' The man's eyes looked tired and he was sinking slowly into his seat. 'It'll chew you up and either spit you out like tar or swallow you up and turn you to stone. Stone. You think I'm joking you? While you're there, you pays the price for the land and shelter. You pays it with your past. It's cursed.' The man took a sip of his drink and then looked deep into Nell's unblinking eyes. 'Cursed by *Mortha Dhagg*,' he spewed in a low growl, before letting out a gravelly snore and falling into a deep sleep. Nell saw Marnie shiver.

At that, the door to The Sky opened. Everyone looked round. Nell closed her eyes, begging the universe, *let it be him!*

'It's blowing a hoolie out there tonight, yessir,' said the barman as he closed the door with his foot and threw a tin plate of kippers on to the table.

Chapter 27

Off Course

PERCY

The sea yanked at Percy's legs, twisted his spine and punched at his ribs. His body woke up with a painful jolt before his brain could work out what was happening.

His arms flailed in all directions; he had no control over his limbs, which now felt long and spindly. For a moment, he was more boy than gilly. In a flash, the sea had become a foreign place. He looked all around him – it was pitch black but for a dot of light swirling maniacally next to him. It was

Connor Price's head torch, in the eye of what appeared to be a huge underwater cyclone.

The sea battled with Percy. He struggled to pull himself away from the cyclone so that he could stop, just for a second, to see clearly what was happening in the eye of the whirlpool. Percy was on the edge of it, and that was bad enough. Even on the periphery, he was being shoved from right to left, up and down in a chaotic scramble. The cyclone battled hard to draw him in.

Too desperate to be fearful, Percy quickly decided what he would have to do. He had two choices: pull himself out of the whirlpool completely and swim clear of its draw, or venture into its heart to try and retrieve his friend.

Gently and slowly, he moved his hands up to his head, where he fought the current in order to turn on his head torch. If he let his arms go wide of his body he was scared the sea would rip them off. With his head torch on, he could see Connor suspended and swirling. He pushed hard with his legs, so hard that he thought his shins might get yanked off at the knee. He hurled his body in, towards the eye of the whirlpool, where Connor was. Connor's body was thrashing about in the swirls and jolts of the cyclone, but he looked disarmingly calm. Percy hoped it was sleep and not death that made his friend look so peaceful.

Percy bravely reached out his arm, even though he really believed that the force of the water might break it, if not something worse. The whirlpool swept him further from the light on Connor's head.

And then, before he really knew what was happening, the cyclone spat him out, an unwanted irritant.

Percy feared it might be a maelstrom. It was powerful, and just big enough to hold both boys in its grip. Percy watched on, helpless, while his friend was twisted and contorted about, still in the eye of the cyclone.

Percy looked around again and noticed that they were close to a wall of rock, just visible in the distance. *Kitterlund*, he dared to think.

This time without fear, Percy pushed forward to the cyclone. He didn't want to think too hard about what he was doing because that would remind him of the danger he was in. He cursed himself for entrusting his life to Connor and the dolphins.

Ignoring the thoughts that told him not to, Percy forced his way in again. He grappled, flailing, until he grabbed

Connor by the arm and pulled him with all the might he could muster. The sea pulled back, drawing Percy in. He fought it, jolting his body back as hard as he could. He heaved Connor from the eye of the cyclone.

He held on to his friend tightly as he swam to the rocks. *What if he's dead, what if I was too late?* Percy tried to push down the thoughts that riddled his mind. It felt like a mile to the rock wall but it was only a few metres away; every kick of his legs was exhausting.

We almost died, we almost died, we almost died.

He didn't let the rush of relief warm his bones too soon though. Even if Connor had somehow managed to defy death, he was surely still within its grip.

When the cyclone fell out of sight, the water became calm. The gentle lapping of the dark water against the rocks, softly swaying them, was surreal. How could the world seem so tranquil and untroubled, when they had been so close to dying only moments ago?

Connor was not safe. He was not awake. Percy could not pull himself and Connor from the water, it was impossible. He was sure that he must've damaged Connor's arm, dislocated it even, as he yanked his friend out of the cyclone. With the sea supporting their weight, Percy held his friend's cheeks in his hands – there was a cut above his eye and Percy could now see, away from the cyclone, a ribbon of blood that was slowly merging into the salty sea around him.

In a panic, Percy screamed. He screamed as loudly as he could to wake his dreaming friend. He opened his mouth and yelled, but the sea mocked him, rendering his fear into a weak, muffled gobble. Bubbles spilled from his frightened jaws. Humans can't make human noises under water. Even those who are only part-human.

It was no good. The salt water of the sea mixed with the salt of Percy's tears. In his heart he thought that Connor was dead, and it had been his job to keep him safe. *Why did he have to follow?* Percy gripped his friend's arms tightly, almost pinching him. He shook Connor as hard as he could.

Connor's eyes opened. The torches cast light only on the boys' faces and the rock wall. Everywhere around them was still black. Connor opened his mouth to scream, but there was no sound. He slowly took in his surroundings and held on to Percy.

The boys tried to pull themselves up the rock face. Percy's head bobbed in and out of the water into the freezing night sky as he lost his footing and was swallowed again by the sea. Clutching precariously at the moss-covered rock, clinging to the seaweed that tangled around their limbs, the boys' beaten bodies were battle-sore. When Percy finally pulled himself up, his words of encouragement to Connor echoed but fell flat, with no other soul to hear them.

Percy stood on the edge of the rock and Connor eventually summoned the strength to tread water next to the stone.

'Give me a minute. I need to get my breath,' panted Connor as he struggled to switch from using his gills to using his shocked and tired lungs.

'I thought you were dead.'

'I nearly was,' said Connor, colour returning slowly to his cheeks as Percy's head torch shone on him, a spot of light in the black of the night and the sea.

'Wait, what's that sound?' whispered Percy urgently.

'It's an echo.'

Percy looked behind him. Beyond the edge of the rock was an entrance into a shallow cave. Percy thought for a moment. 'You need to rest. Let's stay here.'

'I can keep going,' said Connor unconvincingly, his legs still beating in the water.

'It's been three hours since we tethered ourselves to the dolphins. Connor, I think the cyclone loosened us from the tethers and we lost the dolphins then. The water, it's warmer. Look at the sky, it's clear.'

'What about Kitterlund?'

'Kitterlund is long gone.'

Then Percy's face went white.

'What's wrong?' asked Connor quietly. 'What's the matter, Percy? What's—'

'Get out of the water! Get out! Get—' Percy was panicking. He was moving his arms back and forth frantically, gesturing Connor towards him.

Connor was confused, he fumbled at the rock face. He couldn't grip on to anything. His foot was slipping and his arms were too tired to hold the weight of his body.

'Great white!' Percy finally spluttered. Percy threw himself down to his knees at such a speed that they fell hard on the rock and Percy knew immediately that they would be bruised and cut, but the pain would have to wait for later. The fin was getting closer, beginning to circle. His torch lit up the water and Percy could see it, there was no mistaking.

He leant down and gave his arm to Connor and tried with all of his might to pull him out. It wasn't working. 'You have to climb using my arm, Connor, use it like a rope!' With his other arm, Percy held on as tight as he could to a rock that was jutting out next to his foot. The rock was a gift from the sea, curving like a handle into a small rock pool, perfect for Percy to hold on to so that he could gain purchase on its edge. He used his arm and his body as a ballast and slowly, very slowly, Connor made his ascent out of the water.

The boys lay on the rocky ground, exhausted.

'That could've been grizzly,' panted Percy.

Connor tried to laugh, but all he could do was breathe.

The shark circled for a long while. Its fin was exposed, then it disappeared. It returned, then disappeared again, teasing the boys and feeding their fear. Percy and Connor silently watched the shark play its game, not daring to take their eyes off the water.

Connor slowly wiped his brow and looked down at his hand. It was blood-smeared. The shark must have got a taste.

Percy looked down to his knees, which had begun to sting. He'd ignored the discomfort all the time he was trying to save his friend, but now the adrenaline had worn off and he was aware of the pain in his own aching body.

'What will we do if it's still there in the morning?' asked Connor, white as a sheet.

'Open up your bag. We'll build a fire and we'll sleep. We can worry about the shark in the morning.'

The contents of Connor's diving pack mirrored Percy's exactly, and Percy buried the sick feeling of betrayal that rose in the pit of his stomach.

Connor unsealed his box of matches while Percy gathered twigs blown in from an unlikely tree that had somehow managed to establish life at the barren entrance to the cave. They made a fire, but sleep was a long time coming.

Percy worried about the shark. He worried a great deal.

Chapter 28

A Split Second

NELL

The shadow of Marnie's figure woke Nell, who had not slept much. It was only when the sun rose that sleep had finally taken her.

She rubbed her eyes.

'Put on your suit, darling. We have guests,' whispered Marnie.

Nell sat bolt upright. A split second of hope shot through her like an arrow. *Guests? Percy!* But that shortest of moments was cut into two – a brief moment of delight followed by a sinking moment of realisation.

'No, darling, it's not Percy. I'm sorry. But there is something that might cheer you up a little.' Marnie gestured with her hand to starboard.

There, just beneath the surface of the water, was a pod of sea-lions. Nell had drawn a similar sight only days before. *I'll swim with them one day, I know it*, she had thought with a smile.

'Is it safe?' said Nell excitedly as she fumbled with her wet suit, her shivering hands barely able to grip as she pulled it on.

'It's safe, my sweet,' said Marnie, smiling a warm glow.

'We'll be hitting those eddies soon,' warned Otto.

'A few minutes won't make any difference,' Marnie reassured him.

And with the grace of a fish, Nell dived into the cold to join the lions.

The water hit Nell's body with an explosion of cold. Tiny bubbles rose and twisted all around her so that she could not see anything at first. It was an unpleasant shock but then her body tingled with the power of the sea and she felt close to Percy.

The sea-lions looked on in unison as their interloper edged towards them carefully, respectfully. They rolled around and towards Nell, who swam gently to them. A large, smiling sea-lion with the blackest of eyes, so black that they could be deep, deep holes into its soul, swam right up to Nell and nudged her arm. He rolled over on to his back. Nell reached out her hand and stroked his tummy. She tickled it and he contorted in the water, just as Percy would have on the floor in front of the fire as she extracted the remote control from his vice-like grip. The largest sea-lion swam around Nell in a big circle, and the others joined in. They each wanted to be tickled and they showed off their flips and turns to their new friend.

A split second. There was a split second where nothing else mattered – not Mam being so poorly, not school, not Connor's mum and her tears, not missing Goldie and his long arms wrapped around her when she was tired, and not Percy.

But as quickly as it was there, it was gone. Nell closed her eyes, daring, pleading to return to that moment of happiness just one more time, before she would go back to what had become her new reality. But no second moment came.

Nell closed her eyes again and felt the swirl of the water around her as the pinnipeds gently rolled away. She opened her eyes and discovered she was alone but for one sea-lion. The first one. He looked into her eyes, through her goggles.

She took them off. The two were now eye-to-eye and his benevolent expression turned melancholy. And in the black of his gaze she saw something. She stroked him goodbye and swam as fast as she could to the *Mab*.

She pulled herself up the side ladder and on to the deck.

'How was that then, eh?' said Otto.

Nell didn't say a word. She threw off her scuba gear. She didn't even try to peel back her wet suit. She immediately ran downstairs to her sketch-book. Marnie and Otto were left puzzled on the deck as they drew up anchor and hoisted up the main sail.

Nell drew. She drew and she stood back. She knew what it was. But she was too scared to say. So she wrote it instead.

The Dearmad.

Chapter 29

The Birds

NELL

'Well, that must be it – you've drawn it before, but now I am certain...' mumbled Marnie.

'The Dearmad. You got a feelin' about it, old girl?' asked Otto. The three travellers crowded around Nell's drawing.

Nell broke her silence, awoken from the hypnotic hold the picture had over her. She raised her head up so that she could look Marnie in the eye. 'What did he mean, that man, in The Sky? What did he mean when he talked about Mortha Dhagg?'

Otto gave a shiver. He removed his cap, wrung it in his hands and slumped back on to the banquette.

'Mortha Dhagg...' whispered Marnie.

'Do you have to keep saying his name, old girl? He's a hex for us sailors, a hoodoo.' Otto looked uneasy.

'He was a gilly, many many moons ago. When merchants and mercenaries ruled the sea. There were more gillies then. They didn't really mix with humans so much. But not *him*. He was a very wealthy gilly and mixed in the company of wealthy humans. It was a terrible combination,' explained Marnie. 'He used to escort ships, but not like us Shearwaters. It was all about gold, silk, cocoa and spice. Riches. Then people started to notice that the captains of those ships were taking ill, or disappearing altogether. People began to put two-and-two together and realised he was—'

'A pirate?' said Nell.

'I suppose, yes,' said Marnie. 'But, well, gillies were never sure if he was a pirate or something more – perhaps a sorcerer. They feared him, he had a strange power. They say that it was he who discovered Doona. But he was wracked with an extreme greed. He talked about a place in the ocean that held all of the wonders of the world. He talked of it incessantly. A place just for *chosen* gillies.'

'All them non-gillies thought he meant booty, didn't they?' said Otto, shaking his head.

'It was no surprise, then, that word spread. He relented one day, propelled by greed, no doubt, and accepted money to take one merchant there, a very rich man. Mortha Dhagg was promised all the world's riches, a bounty of treasure, all he could ever wish for, in return for safe passage to Doona. But, when they got there, the merchant was so overcome by the beauty and wonder of the island that he refused to leave unless he could take home a tree from its heart. Mortha Dhagg warned him not to, but the merchant ignored him. He dug up a sapling.' Marnie shook her head.

'What happened?' Nell whispered, not taking her eyes off Marnie.

'The ground around the sapling turned black, and was immediately riddled with maggots and snakes that fed on the remnants of the root . The sapling combusted, still in the hand of the merchant's aide, burned to an ember. The crew of the ship fell ill, one by one, until all were dead, and the merchant and his family starved, believing all of the island's food to be tainted.'

Nell's eyes were wide. 'And Percy wants to take something from Doona for Mam?'

Otto shook his head solemnly, eyes cast to the floor.

'Worse still, all gillies paid the price of that merchant's selfish act. Before that day, balance was something that every gilly had in abundance. They were beacons of health. But the strength of Doona was weakened by Mortha Dhagg's actions. Every gilly paid the price.'

'And what about the Dearmad?' asked Nell.

'Mortha Dhagg was so enraged with anger and hatred that he used a curse. Some say he cursed the waters, some say he cursed a cave. The Dearmad. A curse to stop any explorers from reaching Doona.' Marnie sighed and took Nell's picture in her hands. 'Who knows if it's true? Certainly not I! But something does ring true about that cave. The oubliette. I believe it, I believe that the cave is a dangerous place to be, and I think you sense it too, darling.' The cabin fell silent.

With a clatter of wings and squawks, the razorbill suddenly appeared, flying down into the cabin at an extraordinary speed. Feathers fell to the floor as the bird flapped its wings and finally rested on Marnie's wrist.

'The eddies are upon us.' Marnie calmly held the bird and stroked its back. She stared at it, not looking at Nell or Otto.

'Stay here. I may be a few moments,' she whispered, in a trance, as she disappeared up the stairs to the deck of the *Mab*.

Chapter 30

Too Good to be True

PERCY

'Wake up, Connor, come on!' Percy shook Connor's shoulder. His friend's fingers were almost blue. 'Connor! The fire's gone out!'

Connor opened his eyes with a start. 'It's cold.'

'We've got to get out, get moving. Here,' Percy handed his friend a foil pouch of baby food.

'Ugh. No thanks,' said Connor, pushing it away.

'No. Come on. We have to travel even further today. And we're going deeper. Much, much deeper. We might not find any food down there, not food we can trust anyway. Come on!'

Connor slurped up the puréed vegetables with a grimace. 'I regret coming up with *that* idea.'

They stood at the opening of the cave, ready to jump back in.

'It's not here.'

'What?' replied Connor.

'The shark. It's gone,' said Percy.

'Do you really think it was a great white?' asked Connor.

'At the time I thought so, but who knows? Probably not. In these waters, I guess it was more likely a blue shark. But whatever it was, it got a taste for your blood!' said Percy, only realising too late the effect this comment might have on his friend.

Connor looked grey with fear.

'Don't worry, Connor. It won't be back. You're not bleeding now. The salt water has helped you heal and—'

'I know. We can't just stay here. We *have* to do this. Don't we?'

'We do.'

They stood silently. Both boys looked out to the sea. It looked different.

'No waves. Blue sky.' Connor's eyes widened.

'The Doona core ring,' Percy said, with only a little hesitation. 'I'm almost certain. The pull feels different here, it feels stronger. I'd bet that's where we are, wouldn't you?'

'I don't know for sure, but I think you were right last night. The dolphins took us through the eddies, but abandoned us when they hit the cyclone. So it could be true. Maybe we have made it into the Doona core ring without even realising.'

'From now on, we cope on our own. We can't trust anything. We head west – that's the way I feel it, so that's the way we'll go.'

'I feel that too.'

The boys smiled at one another. Hitching their knees to their chests, they bombed into the water, screaming at the top of their lungs, 'DOONA!'

* * *

The boys swam deep. They went far, far below the surface of the sea. Through kelp and plankton, through tribes of herring. Through fish that they recognised vaguely from the library but which real life had hidden from them until now. The whirlpool had churned up nutrients from the deep that were feeding all manner of wild and wonderful creatures.

They went deeper still, eager to go faster. Connor had found his stride and was becoming a stronger swimmer despite the tiredness that had struck his body before. Had Percy thought about it, it might have been the first tell-tale sign that they were indeed on the Doona core ring. Doona was already working its magic on Connor Price.

With their torches on, the boys saw a huge bloom of jelly-fish lit up far away in the distance.

A killer whale swam by, hunting a shoal of herring.

At one time Percy would have been wide-eyed and stunned, excited at the beauty and grace but also the danger of being this close to such a magnificent predator. But it felt normal. This place, filled with life, was becoming home. They would be OK. They hung back and watched, changed course – not out of fear, but out of respect. Percy was learning which instincts to trust. Percy felt sure that they would be OK.

Connor and Percy began to approach what looked like the sea bed coming up towards them. They slowed down, turning to each other, shocked. It was covered by magical, luminous soft coral and painted anemones swaying with the ebb and flow. The invertebrates caught plankton on the currents of the pure water; the boys could feel the water feeding them too.

Percy could taste it in his gills. If Doona had purer waters than these he could not even imagine what they could do for him, for Connor, for Mam.

The water here was undamaged by the chug and churn of the marina and the waste that clogged the lifeblood of the sea at home. Port Kipneash was considered to have the purest of waters, perfect for gillies. Percy felt cheated by that empty promise. Cheated on behalf of his mam. Mam deserved better. She deserved *this*. He'd never experienced anything like it before.

The boys feasted on the plants and crustaceans that they recognised from their studious preparations. Connor chewed on a piece of red seaweed and gazed into the anemones with a happy, full tummy. Percy laughed as a well-disguised king crab, hidden perfectly amongst the anemones, twitched and then slowly sidled sideways, away from Connor.

This was joy, this was their habitat. It was where they were supposed to be. Nowhere else on earth could possibly be better – how could Doona beat this?

They carried on their journey as if they had not a fear in the world. The waters of the Doona core ring made them stronger, they swam faster; they could carry on for hours without feeling tired or hungry, they took on a superhuman gilly strength, unimpinged by the trappings of life as a human. They were on their way. This was the gateway to Doona.

It was all going to be fine.

It was.

Chapter 31

The Ocean Deep and Wide

NELL

Soon after the razorbill entered the cabin of the *Mab*, the sky grew angry and Otto confirmed that he could see the currents in the distance. The *Mab* rocked viciously and Nell thought she saw something resembling fear in Otto's eyes.

'Every one of them tales was copper-bottomed in its telling...' muttered Otto.

'Copper-bottomed?' questioned Nell, who had thought she was getting used to Otto's strange way of talking.

'True. Them tales was *true*,' Otto said, without taking the binoculars from his eyes. 'Them currents go on for miles, I tell ya... I see no end to 'em,' said Otto in awe as he strained to see through his binoculars where the swirling patterns might end.

'So we can't we just go around them?' asked Nell innocently.

'There ain't no goin' round 'em. No, this is where they says you's gotta pass. If we does a detour now, just to avoid the eddies, we'll never get back on to the route. And without a gilly guiding us... well, the odds is stacked against us, anyway.'

The razorbill was perched regally on the balustrade, and an enormous, powerful-looking albatross glided overhead, wings so wide they felt like a shelter.

'Wait here for one hour, Otto,' commanded Marnie. 'Go no further. There is more clement weather ahead.' She raised her hands in a salute to the brooding sky above her.

Under strict instructions to remain below deck, Marnie and Nell could feel the chill of the grey and angry sky as they looked up through the open cabin hatch. But the sea was not fighting them any more. The waters were settling.

After a time of waiting, a shard of almost blinding sunlight appeared to burst through the clouds above them. The boat ploughed forward, almost effortlessly. It was just as Marnie had said – the weather was now on their side.

'Well, this is unheard of! I was hoping for at least a bit of truck to tell the lads about when I got me old bones back home!' Otto called down to them.

Nell shot a confused look at Marnie. 'Truck?' she said as she stood at the foot of the cabin stairs, peering up to get a glimpse of Otto, who was jumping about, rubbing his head and muttering to himself.

'He means truculence, from the sea.' Marnie grinned as she dipped a biscuit in her tea. 'Don't worry my love, we'll have you fluent in Otto-speak in no time at all.'

'If Mam were here, she'd say you look very pleased with yourself, Marnie.'

'Do I? I suppose I have my uses.'

Before Nell could ask any questions, Otto was calling to them again.

'What? What is this madness? The birds, Marnie! Your birds are here. They're all over the deck!' they heard Otto shout. There was a clatter on the deck and then Nell could barely hear Otto above the squawks and calls of the birds who had gathered on and around the deck of the *Mab*. 'The starlings is back! All over the boat they is!'

'Shall we come up, Otto? Do you need help?' Nell called to Otto.

'Wait where you is... Here it comes, we're hitting our first eddy now!'

Nell and Marnie held to the sides of the banquette, but within a few short moments, the swaying stopped and the *Mab* was still again.

'This just ain't right!' Nell could hear Otto say, over and over, while Marnie smiled contentedly to herself. 'What the... the birds... Marnie, what the heck is going on with these birds? They're menacing me!' Otto called.

'They aren't doing any such thing,' muttered Marnie. 'They're just friendly.'

'Oh, hello little fella.' Nell heard Otto talking to one of the birds. 'Watch I don't stand on you there, little one!'

'I think they're getting under his feet now.' Marnie chuckled.

'Can I go up and see?' asked Nell.

'Best leave Otto to it, I think.'

They hit seven more eddies, and with each one, Otto gave a running commentary of the birds and their menacing ways. Nell and Marnie clung tight to the banquette where they sat.

Finally, Otto trundled down into the cabin and dropped his cap wearily on the table. 'I gotta say, that was the strangest bit of sea-faring I has ever done, in all my years... It was too easy. It don't feel right. Did them birds have something to do with this, old girl? I could see them eddies coming, but it weren't nearly as bad as all them stories would have you believe. I swear them birds was guiding us through...'

'What can I say? I'm a good friend of the sky,' Marnie smiled, shrugged and winked at Nell.

* * *

Days passed, the sea ebbed and flowed, and no news was certainly not good news.

It had been nine days since they last saw home. Nine days since their feet last touched Jetty Beach. Nine days and there had been no sign of Percy or Connor.

They were well within the core ring. The seas were unusually calm, and none of Otto's tools for reading the tides, the flows of the sea, the pressures of the air, were working. The pin of the compass spun and spun in utter confusion. To say Otto was unsettled would be an understatement.

'This is unheard of! Unheard of I tell you! It's bafflements. It truly is.'

'We've got good intentions, Otto dear *hombre*. Good intentions go a long way.' Marnie said in a reassuring tone.

'Aye. You are right. Maybe that's why the sea don't seek to fox us today.'

Nell was frustrated by the riddles Otto and Marnie spoke in, but she was relieved that they had somehow made it through the eddies unscarred.

Another night passed and another morning was upon them with nothing ahead but the sea... and the razorbill.

And then things started to become very odd indeed.

On the morning of their tenth day at sea, the albatross returned. It seemed like the same one that had been there on the day they passed through the eddies, but Nell couldn't be sure. At first, Marnie welcomed the bird, but the razorbill made strange squawking noises until Marnie eventually took him below deck and left the albatross feasting on crackers fed to it by Otto.

And then, on this morning of their tenth day at sea, Otto began behaving very strangely too. He was all of a sudden short tempered and mumbled to himself incessantly. Nell could not make out a word he was saying.

'Otto,' Nell said as she sidled up to her captain. He looked shorter somehow. 'Is everything all right? You don't seem yourself today.' Otto ignored her. He looked straight ahead. 'Otto?'

Still no answer.

'Otto!' Nell shouted, growing impatient.

'Quiet!' he hissed, his eyes looked red, wet and wild. His cap fell off as he turned quickly to Nell. The few wisps of hair that he had left were pointing in all directions.

She followed the direction of his eyes and froze. She was too scared to let herself believe what she was looking at. It was right in front of them.

'That's it, isn't it.' It was not a question.

It wasn't like the other islets they had passed after Kitterlund. Nell had swum up to each one to check for signs of Percy; each was a disappointment. The rock that lay ahead of them was not like those. Tall, it pointed majestically out of the sea, up to the heavens, as if reaching up to be set free.

'Look at your watch.'

Nell looked at her watch. The second hand wasn't moving. Otto held out his own pocket watch that was connected by a chain to his dungarees. It showed the same time as Nell's.

'The clocks have stopped.' Otto looked at Nell, waiting to see if she understood what this meant. 'Get your book. Get it, my girl.'

Otto and Marnie followed Nell down to the cabin, and sat at the table as she quickly turned the pages of her book. She hesitated, stopped and lay the book flat. Her pencil strokes showed a cave, the cave she'd seen in the sea lion's eyes. At first she'd thought it was a man's face – it started that way. But the crevices of age became deeper and deeper and the old, sagging eyes turned black and eventually disappeared under the graphite. The heavy brows remained as indents in the great, looming rock. Nell could still see the face. She knew what it was when she drew it.

'The cave is inside that islet. I know it,' she murmured.

Marnie clasped her hand around Nell's and gasped. '*The Dearmad*. You drew the Dearmad.'

'We are near it, girl. Time be disappearing.'

'We won't all be able to go in. It's too great a risk. One of us must go at a time. I nominate myself first. I will go, and if the Dearmad takes me, Otto, you must come,' said Marnie, with eyes fixed on Nell's drawing.

'No! No, no, no!' shouted Nell without a second's hesitation. 'I can do this. I *have* to do this. Don't you understand? I *know*

201

that he's in there. He won't go with you, he won't! I know that cave has started to work its evil on him. Don't you see? The only one of us with any chance of bringing him back is *me*.'

She turned the page slowly and there, clear as rock, was Percy, stood in the Dearmad. She had drawn this one in colour, but Percy's eyes were black, blank, and he was surrounded by stalagmites and stalactites. There was a deep pool just next to where he stood, emerald green in parts, a beautiful pale blue in others. Even on the page, it glistened with an iridescent magic. It was beyond inviting. Connor was swimming happily in it. A great shard of light was darting in from above. Nell was sat at the edge of the pool.

'I've seen it. *I* am the one that goes in. *I* am the only one who can save my twin.'

'Is this a premonition?' asked Marnie.

'I don't know. I think it is, but I don't really know how all this works. I mean, as strange as it sounds, I believe it's a premonition. Yes.' Nell nodded .

'Do you know that you will succeed? Have you seen it?'

Nell shook her head. 'I haven't seen it. But I feel it.'

'Then I suppose you must go,' Marnie said with a tremor in her voice. 'I believe in your pictures. I believe it has to be you.' A tear rolled down her cheek.

'But the birds...' began Otto.

'My birds are only half the story. Nell is the only one who can retrieve him if he is... If...' the words seemed to stick in Marnie's throat, too awful to speak out loud.

Otto simply looked down and shook his head.

'If we go first, it won't just be her brother she'll need to save. She'll have to save two old idiots too.'

Marnie broke a smile. Otto smiled too. Neither of them looked happy.

'The girl's got grit,' said Otto, as if Nell had already gone.

Chapter 32

The Dearmad

PERCY

Percy woke up. He sat upright in his bed.

A bed.

A real bed!

Well, a tattered camp-bed. But at least it was not the sea bed.

He allowed the thought to melt away before he could wonder again what wreckage had delivered the beds to the cave, or what had happened to the cave's previous inhabitants to make them abandon their wares.

A thick shard of light flowed through the cave. He followed the shard up with his eyes. A great hole loomed over him and through it he saw a bright light-blue sky. A bird flew over, clearly not tempted to enter. The cave was tall. Taller than he could ever imagine a cave being. Still, it felt like home.

Above him were the longest, most beautiful stalagmites and stalactites he had ever seen; multi-coloured rock in varied and magical tones of purple, blue, red and green. Some pointed down at him like arrows pointing towards a curiosity in a zoo. *Come here! Look here! Here he is!* they cried out.

There was the familiar lapping of the sea, but Percy could hear a deep hum too. It was the swill of the gentle wind in the cave; it sounded both hollow and deep at the same time, it was musical and it was dull. The ting-ting-ting of a wind chime played in time with the bass-tone drum of the air rolling around the crevices of the cave. An echoing drip sounded like the melodic tick-tock of a clock.

Percy looked around the camp. There were three beds, one was his. One would be Connor's. Yes, Connor was with him. That was familiar.

'Sea booty!' a voice echoed suddenly.

Percy was relieved; he didn't like being alone... it was a sensation that felt somehow alien to him... like there had always been someone there before, and the absence of them now was unsettling... It was a sensation that he found hard to untangle.

'It's the good stuff!' the voice called again.

Although Percy was pleased to hear the voice calling to him because it meant he was no longer alone, he had a feeling in the pit of his stomach that *this* was not the voice he wanted to hear. That the voice he really wanted to hear belonged to a girl...

Percy followed the sound of the voice calling to him. 'Connor,' he whispered to himself. *That's Connor.*

Connor was treading water in the deep pool at the centre of the cave. He had a fistful of bright green seaweed and he was holding it up in the air for Percy to see. Percy wandered over and looked over the side, and saw that it was a steep climb to get out of the water. Connor was nimble though, moving his feet and hands from one protruding stone to another; he'd done this before. The pool held the lightest, bluest water that Percy had ever seen or imagined; it was clear and beautiful and, looking into its depths, he saw it was full of small fish and seaweed perfect for plucking.

The tick-tocking drip, drip, drip sound was coming from behind him. It was a fresh water trickle dropping into a tin bucket. Percy suddenly felt overwhelmingly thirsty so he rushed to the bucket and lapped at the water like a dog.

'We've got cups!' Connor laughed.

'Where have you been?'

'In the pool, it's amazing. I reckon that's how we got in here – I think it leads to the sea.'

'That makes sense. Did you find the way out?'

Connor stopped with a start. He stared at Percy. A flash of horror covered his face. 'No. I wasn't looking for a way *out*.'

The boys gorged on the seaweed that Connor had plundered from the pool. They lay in the beam of sunlight, resting their bones on blankets which were laid out on the rocks. They had discovered a nook inside the cave which had been transformed into a cupboard, complete with shelves, and full of books. Books upon books about the sea, sea life, tales of the sea. Percy read and dreamed, only occasionally stopping to wonder where the books had come from, and how they happened to be in the cave. Such thoughts were fleeting and scurried from his mind as quickly as they burst into it. The idea of *previous residents* never occupied either boy's thoughts for very long.

They found a ball and played a strange version of football that involved the walls of the cave and the pool, and goals made out of piles of old dusty cans they had found hidden under the planks of a makeshift kitchen.

There was a chute on the other side of the pool; they guessed it was for rubbish and threw all the old fish bones and shells down it, listening carefully for a splash or plop, but all they heard was the bang-bang-bang of bone on rock.

The day was filled and it was empty, and the boys talked only of what was there, what was around them, their new world, nothing of what had been before. It felt so normal to Percy. There were a few small trees and shrubs that grew within the cave, thriving despite their unlikely settling-place amongst the stone and rock. One tree in particular gave Percy an unnerving feeling every time he went near it; a feeling that there was somewhere he was meant to be... something he should have done. And there were other unusual feelings too; when he saw a bird fly over the cave he would instinctively reach out as if he could touch it. He longed for them to come closer, but he couldn't be sure why.

They didn't think about Doona or home, the place they had come from or the place they were going to. They didn't think about the people left behind or why they were there. Their whole world existed only in the cave.

The light dimmed and they lit a fire with some ancient matches they magpied from the kitchen, and twigs blown in through the cavity in the ceiling of their cave. Their home. Their home that had been someone else's home before them, littered with souvenirs and relics from dwellers past. Books and blankets. Tins and cutlery.

Tired and peaceful, Connor drifted to sleep. Percy held his knees to his chest and noticed grazes; they were faded. He wondered how they came to be there, what had happened? Where had he been? He looked at his hands, and something like a memory began to build; it felt unfamiliar, odd, like it was precious and could melt away at any moment. An image flashed through his mind: he was sat on the edge of a bed, in a room, in a house, snipping his nails with small, round-edged scissors. That must have been at least two weeks ago; his nails would need a cut soon, they always grew fast. He thought of the ashes from the fire – a great pile had been building.

As his eyelids grew heavy, the last thing he saw was a tally of four white lines scratched with stone on to the rock next to his bed. Without thinking, he picked up a stone from the floor and struck them out with his own line. Five. And as his eyes blinked shut with sleep, he had a strange sensation that he had done this before.

Chapter 33

Nell and the Mouth of the Dearmad

NELL

'Now listen, *guapa*, keep your head about you. You are strong, *fuerte*, true?' Marnie was coaching Nell.

Nell nodded. She didn't feel *fuerte*, but she nodded anyway.

'Keep your sketch-pad with you. Keep drawing. Keep drawing, all the time. It will help you to remember. Keep thinking of us. Keep thinking of your mam and Goldie. Keeping your premonitions in order might help to keep your memories safe too. Think of us all the time. You hear me?

All. The. Time,' repeated Marnie. 'The cave can only *hide* us. What is hidden is not lost. We will be there.' And then, quite out of nowhere and quite viciously, she tugged hard on Nell's earlobe, pinching as she did.

'Ow! All right!' Nell knew that she had to feel this advice. She needed to feel it like a prod to the head. But it didn't make it any easier to digest.

Otto looked edgy; he shuffled from one foot to the other, looking to Marnie for reassurance. Then, in one swift, sudden movement, Otto joined in and gave Nell a jab in the arm with his finger.

'Hey!' Nell yelped, now rubbing her arm too.

'Oh, my little lady, you gotta forgive me.' He jumped on the spot, wrung his hat, biting his lip as he did. 'It's just, when you goes into that place, I hopes you can still *feel* us, if you needs to feel us.' Otto blushed, he was unused to hurting anyone, least of all a child.

Nell understood. She rubbed the spot where a bruise would surface.

'Well, if you've finished beating me up, I'd better be gone.' Nell climbed on to the side of the boat while they lifted on her scuba gear. 'But not for long.'

She picked up her small diving pack containing her sketchbook and pencils, and secured it carefully around her chest. Not able to speak with her scuba gear on, she reached forward and stroked Marnie's face and then Otto's. Then, looking into Otto's eyes, she gave him a dead-arm.

Nell slid quickly into the water.

Taking advantage of the fact that she was wearing her full scuba gear, she swam as deep as she could manage. Nell had always adored the ocean, but it hadn't chosen her; its true wonder had always been out of reach. But, alone in these waters, everything felt different. If she ignored for a moment the sound of her own breathing, loud in her scuba mask, and the weight of the tank on her back, she could dream that she was a gilly too.

Nell shook her head. *Stay focused*, she reprimanded herself. She battled the urge to become a tourist, to indulge in the awe and wonder; she couldn't afford the time to be mesmerised by the shock of fluorescent colours, the anemones, the rare hotchpotch collection of fish she had never seen before. A tight school of lined catfish swam by, at least a hundred, all huddled in a ghostly, swaying pyramid, lurking, looking for food. Nell treated the sight like it was old news. A goliath grouper looked at her curiously, its bulbous lips munching on the remnants of a lobster. It was as long as Goldie was tall, but Nell barely gave it a second glance.

And there was a clatter of noise in the sea too. She could just about hear it over her own noisy breathing and the creak of her wet suit. The bubbling, gurgling noise of movement was punctuated by the clickety-clack screeching of fish chatting away. Maybe it was dolphins. There was no time to investigate.

In the distance, just beyond the side of the cave, there was a huge drop in the level of the sea bed, like an underwater canyon or gully. She felt nervous as she looked towards it. She chose to follow the path towards the rock. Who knew what kind of murky dangers lay beneath? A shiver trembled all the way through her body as she was reminded that she did not know what kind of murky dangers lay ahead of her, either.

It felt like the sea was gently pulling her towards the gully, urging her towards it, quietly calling her in. She kept her course.

Finally, the sea bed rose to meet her as the ominous rock got closer. On the craggy sea floor, where the outer wall of the cave merged with the rock and sand of the sea bed, lay several unfeasibly huge bones. They existed here as discarded sea booty, lying on the sea bed touched only by the clams, barnacles and ebb of the sea. But who knew where they came from? And there were signs of human life too. Something was sticking out from the sand beneath her feet. At first she wondered if she had spied a particularly alien-looking fish wearing a transparent floatation device around its belly. Or perhaps it was a half-fish-half-jellyfish creature? But no. On closer inspection she saw that she was looking at the top of a glass bottle, with the head of a little mosshead warbonnet peeking out of it. The only reason she could identify this most unusual fish, with feather-like plumes jutting from its head, was that Mam had shown her a picture of one. Mam said it looked like Arnie, the local mechanic who overcharged but always did a good job. Nell recognised it instantly. The bottle was covered in bright pink mossy growths, making the mosshead's home look very inviting indeed.

As she surveyed the rocks, thinking of her exit route and what lay ahead, when she would be on dry land, her attention was brought swiftly back to the sea and the world that existed only beneath the waves. A giant octopus swam past her and snatched the shiny aluminium water bottle that had been hanging from the waistband of her wet suit. The octopus was huge and orange, and its massive fleshy head looked like it was made from crinkled, wet crepe paper. Its eyes were barely open and it had an air of audacious confidence that made Nell laugh, once she recovered from the sheer shock of its size. The magnificent creature was four metres long at least, and its tentacles reached out far and wide. Without thinking, Nell swam up and snatched the water bottle back, thinking *I'll have that back, thank you very much*. It was Goldie's bottle and there was no way she was going to lose it.

As Nell approached the cave, tentatively, she knew something was amiss. The sea was still, calm like it had been for days now. An eerie calm. There had been islets that were far too treacherous for Nell to swim close to. She always treated the white foam with caution; it was an indicator that the sea had been playing its cat-and-mouse game of chase, making the waters wild. The *Mab* had sailed quietly past those caves with their crashing waves and monstrously sharp rocks, while her three passengers hoped that Percy had passed them by too.

But as they had gone deeper into the Doona core ring, the sea had changed. It became unnervingly calm. And this cave was even calmer still. The sea lapped gently around the rock, quietly inviting her closer.

Lifting her head into the open air, she swam close to the rock, surveying its contours. She had found the way in – the mouth of the cave. She heaved her body, adorned as it was with all her cumbersome equipment, out of the water. Immediately, and with a disappointment that swelled like the ocean in the pit of her stomach, she could see that the cave was empty. No Percy. No Connor. Not only that, it was only a few metres deep; there was nothing inside.

This isn't The Dearmad, it can't be, it's just a lump of stupid rock! she raged to herself. *But what if... This cave is cursed. Don't trust it. You can't trust it.* She jumped back into the water. She swam around what at first had looked like the cave entrance, but this time with a more cautious eye.

She knew that there would be trickery.

Maybe it was a puzzle.

Could there be a way in if she swam back to the gully she had seen under the water? That dark hole of a canyon that she had been scared of before... Even the idea of underwater cave systems made her feel queasy. It would be so easy to get trapped. Lost forever. Those voids that brave divers swam through had always scared her. But she knew that Percy was used to swimming through them. She wasn't about to give up. *One last try in the cave. And then the gully. So be it.*

She pulled herself up on to the rock floor and looked in each nook and cranny. She was desperate to find a way in that did not involve an underwater route. Her oxygen was depleting, minute by minute. And what if it was another false alarm, another trick of the rock? The gully had to be her last resort. It was such a risk.

She heard a voice. It was a young voice. *It might be Percy*, she dared hope. Or maybe Connor. It was too distant to tell.

'Hello!' she yelled.

Nothing.

'Percy!'

Nothing.

She stood still, trying desperately to hear the sounds again. She peeled back her wet suit, which clung to her skin, and she lifted off her heavy scuba gear. She hid both in one of the nooks of the cave. She lifted on her rucksack and stood still again, leaning her body forward, as if this would help her to hear.

Nothing.

Then, *CRASH*! A pile of clam shells rained down just a few steps from where she was stood. She hadn't paid it any attention before, but there was a scattering of shells and fish bones along with some rusted and rotting cans on the floor of the cave.

There, in the darkest corner, was a rubbish chute.

Shielding her face with her arm, Nell tentatively looked up. It could only be five metres to the top, and she could see a small light shining down. Someone, or some*thing*, was living up there, that was clear. But the warm wave of hope that rippled through her body soon turned to ice, and she shivered as reality set in. The ascent was vertical, and narrow, with too few footholds to even attempt to climb it alone. She would never make it to the top.

And then she spied a second dot, the smallest possible shard of light a few metres beyond the chute, in a tiny enclave within the shallow cave. She crawled over a pile of old fish bones and clam shells, trying in vain not to slash her knees on the razor-sharp edges of the prickly debris.

Just beyond the drop from the rubbish chute, there was a second tunnel. This one was not a steep chute but a winding and gradual tunnel. She would fit. She could certainly crawl along it.

Without a second thought, she entered the tunnel and crawled as fast as she could through the cold, rocky stone.

The intestines of the Dearmad... what a place to get stuck. She tried not to think about it. The tunnel was black as night, but after a few metres of crawling at a slow incline, heart racing, breathing faster with nerves as much as exertion, it began to grow lighter.

A dim blurring of light was starting to give colour to the deep dark of the rocky tunnel and Nell could see the beautiful mottled stone in all its different hues. The light grew brighter and brighter the further she went. Her skin brushed silently against the cold rock every time she miscalculated a move. This crawl would be painted on her body with bruises, scrapes and scuffs. But she did not flinch. She knew that she was nearly at the end.

She sat still. The rest was vertical now. Up, up, up. Three metres between Nell and the end. A ladder would be handy, but without one she would need to wedge herself in, hold on to the sides and inch herself up.

Or she could call up for a rope.

She froze.

What if he wasn't there?

And if it was him, what should she do? He might not know who she was. A tear rolled down her cheek and she wiped it quickly and unceremoniously away with the fleshy ball of her hand.

'I'm going for a swim, Percy, fish supper!'

'OK! I'll get the fire going...'

It was them. It was certainly, without any question or shadow of a doubt, them.

She could hear them as clearly as if they were stood next to her.

She was frozen still.

'Hello? Percy!' she called up. 'Hello?' she called again, a little louder this time.

A face appeared at the top of the tunnel above her head. It was Percy. It was unmistakeably Percy. He was there, at the top of a tunnel in the middle of the ocean. Just there, looking down at her with a great big vacant smile on his face. The smile of a polite stranger. He was looking at her like she was a new girl at school. He had no idea who she was.

'Need a hand?'

Chapter 34

Nice to Meet You, I'm Your Sister

NELL

Nell scrambled up the tunnel by gaining a foothold on an elbow-high rock, while Percy reached down to pull her up.

'Have you been there long?' asked Percy, as if sitting silently in a tunnel was the most normal thing in the world.

'Oh no, not long. I was, um, I was just taking a swim outside the cave and thought I would come and explore.'

Percy looked distracted. He was staring at Nell's knees. Nell looked down.

'Oh, my legs, yes, they're bleeding. That tunnel is really rocky.' She chuckled nervously.

'Come and sit down. I think there are some plasters around here. Or there are some bandages in my bag...' Percy wandered off. Nell looked all around her, the cave was impressive. In fact, it was remarkable.

It was early evening and she could see the stars in the darkening sky through the cavity in the cave's roof. Though beautiful, the night was unforgiving. And, away from the fire, the coldness of the cave riddled her bones.

'Wow, did you bring all of this stuff with you?' asked Nell, indicating towards the beds, the books, the blankets, as she sat by the boys' small fire.

Percy looked back at her blankly.

'No, it belongs here. This stuff belongs here,' Connor called over. He was busy gutting fish into the pool, barely acknowledging her arrival.

'I guess sailors who have stopped here have just left things for other people to use. That's pretty kind, isn't it?' Nell said.

'Hmm, I suppose so,' said Percy as he put a plaster on the biggest graze on Nell's left knee. 'There, that should help stop the bleeding.'

'Thank you.' Nell smiled. She pulled out some joggers and a T-shirt from her diving pack. She hoped Percy would recognise her *Happy Holidays in Port Kipneash* tee. But he didn't. She put them on over her swimsuit and sat back on the bed. Connor walked over and placed two large fish on a rack that was suspended over the fire.

'That's my bed,' he grunted.

'Oh, sorry, I didn't realise.' Nell bristled. She recalled all the times over the last weeks when Connor had taken *her* place by the fire after swimming. All the times that she'd woken up to the sound of him having breakfast at the Shearwater dinner table. She bit her lip.

'You can have that one.' Connor pointed towards a bed made from a metal frame and a taut piece of fabric, fraying and beige with dirt. It stood less than half a metre from the cold stone floor of the cave.

Even in her drawings, Nell had never anticipated the Dearmad would be so magical, so expansive. It was festooned with shadows like human figures, painting their stories on the walls. Ragged in patches, smooth in others, its formations were twisted and looked as if they had once grown like flowers. And the pool in the centre of the cave was the lightest, most iridescent blue. Even in the cold of night it looked like it was calling Nell in to swim.

By candlelight, Percy pulled out an old blanket from behind a rock. He put it around Nell's shoulders. It was woollen, scratchy, and smelled of the sea.

Never forgetting the outside world, Nell mapped out the cave in her mind's eye. There was quite a jump down into the pool, and they were undoubtedly several metres above sea level if the level of the water was anything to go by. She tried not to think about what would happen to the tunnel if the water rose with the tides; she didn't much like the idea of having to flee the cave through a flooded tunnel – not without her scuba gear.

'Thanks.' She smiled at her brother as he sat back down.

'You're lucky,' said Percy, smiling too, oblivious.

'Am I?'

'Yes, we all are. To live here.'

'Where else could we live? Do you remember where you lived before here?' asked Nell, seizing her opportunity.

Connor jumped to his feet. 'Look at our stalactite.' He gestured upwards. 'I reckon it's the biggest in the world, and it has a fresh-water drip – listen!' Nell listened to the sound of water dripping on metal. 'That's the water bucket.'

'And we've got more food than you could ever eat.' Percy smiled.

'Where does the food come from?'

'The pool, of course! We get everything from the pool. Seaweed, mussels, fish, squid. The works. There are crystals growing in the pool. Big shiny ones.'

'That stalactite, there, hanging, in the rock...' began Nell.

'Yes?' Connor said hesitantly.

'Well, I've seen bigger ones. In different caves. Have you seen other caves?'

The boys looked at Nell blankly.

No, because that would require memory, thought Nell sarcastically.

'Food's nearly ready. It's your turn to clean up after dinner tonight, don't forget,' Connor said to Nell, curtly.

'How can it be my turn? I've only just arrived.'

The boys laughed. 'You're funny!' Percy grinned and slapped Nell gently on the back, congratulating her on the apparently hilarious joke she had made.

This was bad. Really bad. They were forgetting what had happened a matter of minutes ago. It was so much worse than Nell had imagined it could be.

She didn't ask the boys who they thought had brought the beds to the cave, or what had happened to the cave's previous inhabitants. And she didn't bother to ask what they would do when their matches ran out, or when they could find no more twigs blown in by the wind. Burning the branches of the few plants that had endeavoured to grow within the walls of the cave was a short-term plan; there was not an infinite supply.

Nell knew that her questions would all be met with that peculiar blank expression the boys had worn since she arrived. Getting them to leave was not going to be easy.

'My boat is docked just outside the cave...' Nell started. 'How long have you been here?' Nell tried in vain to make the boys think back.

'You ask a lot of questions,' grunted Connor as he wandered off to peer into the pool. She noticed that he did that an awful lot – stare creepily into the pool.

Nell's bed was next to Percy's, and Connor's was a little way past them, on the other side of the fire. The cave was nowhere near as comfy as the boat. The way Connor had talked about the beds you would think they were made of the smoothest and firmest mattresses, made to order, with goose feather duvets, and washed in the soapiest sweet-smelling suds. But there was no mattress, or duvet. If Nell rolled over in the night, the camp-bed would certainly collapse.

She looked at Percy as he lay down. Above his bed, she saw the white lines.

She stared.

It made no sense.

He clearly couldn't remember anything before the Dear-mad. He still didn't know who she was. But a tally? Surely a tally meant that he was aware of time passing. Nell was filled with hope. She smiled. Percy looked over and he smiled back, a smile that she recognised.

And with that, Nell fell to sleep, unsure what the morning would bring.

Chapter 35

The Birds

NELL

The sun rose and set above the cave four times. Still the Dearmad was not winning its battle with Nell. The names and faces of the ones she loved had not been stolen from her. But she was not unafraid.

With her appetite gone, Nell was left with a constant sick feeling in her stomach. Her teeth chattered but her skin was hot to touch. She kept the people and memories she was trying to protect at the fore of her thoughts, but this only made the cave more difficult to bear. She missed home so much that she would hide beneath her blanket to cry, pretending to be asleep.

'Morning, Connor.' She sniffed, trying to muster enthusiasm. 'What's for breakfast? Hot chocolate and muffins? Toast and marmalade? Sausage sandwiches with lashings of tomato ketchup?' she asked, facetiously. Connor looked up, reactionless, from the red seaweed and sardines that he was stirring in a pan over the fire. 'It hasn't rained again,' she said, nodding at the empty tin bucket.

Connor looked confused. 'Oh that thing,' he said, 'that's what we collect our drinking water in.'

'Yes, I know,' said Nell, exasperated. 'But there's been no rain, so let's hope we have some today, hey? You gillies will get ill without at least a little fresh water, won't you?'

'Yes. Good idea,' said Connor, confused.

The lack of drinking water had been all Connor had spoken about the day before. But he had forgotten. Nell would need to start weaving her tangled web of deception again. It was a lie she had concocted; the boys could last long periods with only sea water. Weeks even. But Nell could not. She'd pilfered the small amount that came into the cave each night, sneaking it into Goldie's shiny water bottle while the boys were distracted or asleep, so that the bucket always appeared empty.

The slow, frustrating, boring rumble of life in the Dearmad made Nell lethargic and despondent. She fidgeted and huffed. All she wanted was to leave.

'I've found a carving in the stone!' called Percy as he inspected the walls of the cave, again.

'You found that one yesterday,' murmured Nell under her breath. It wasn't easy to miss. It looked like a man, sat hunched with his elbows on his knees, just next to their campbeds. It gave Nell shivers.

'What's that you're doing?' asked Percy in a rare moment of curiosity.

'I'm writing the names of my family in the dust. Do you know these names?'

'Ha! That's funny. You're funny.' He laughed before running off to kick an empty can around with Connor.

As Nell looked up to the bright blue sky above her head, and wrapped the harsh woollen blanket around her cold bones and sweating skin, she began to think of action. She had to *do* something. Just being here was not enough. And, as if the world agreed with her, something happened.

She saw the razorbill circling over the cave. She was not sure at first, as the top of the cave was so far up. It swooped and dived and circled, tentatively, around the cavity in the cave's roof. It flew back and forth for several minutes and Nell willed it to come in.

Eventually, the bird summoned the courage to make a dive. It swooped elegantly, gently, to Nell's side. A tiny piece of paper made into a scroll encased the bird's fragile leg. It hopped closer and Nell untwined the note, being careful not to harm the bird's delicate body. She flattened the paper out on the bunk.

The birds are watching and bringing us news.
There has been no change so we must consider a new plan.
Please come back to us now.

Nell wrapped her arm round her body to find the place where Otto had poked her. The bruise had faded to nothing, but if she pressed down on her flesh she could still feel the smart of Otto's jab. The memories were intact.

She leant down for her bag and grappled for her book, acting quickly before the razorbill made its flight back. Its feet were beginning to jump a little; it shivered and puffed out its feathers. The bird was agitated.

'Wait, wait, please!' She tore a small strip of paper from her book and wrote,

I'm OK. Need more time.

Baked beans for supper tomorrow night? Prepare enough for five.

She rolled it as tightly as she could around the razorbill's leg. She closed her eyes and screwed up her face, trying to muster the same positivity that she had faked for her note.

'I've been there!' said a voice next to her. In her rush to send off her note, Nell had not noticed Percy sidle up to her and turn the page of her book. He was looking at the room below the deck of the *Mab*. Otto and Marnie were sat at the table having a cup of tea. It was not one of Nell's best, but she had been happy with the likeness of Marnie in particular.

Nell felt like she was holding a precious pressed flower by a single petal. A slight breeze now could destroy this moment completely. This was her chance.

'Yes. You have been there, Percy. Not so long ago. Do you think you might know those people?'

'Hmm. I think—' Percy started. But he was stopped short.

'What's going on?' Connor appeared by the bunk, hands on his hips, feet spread out. He looked so different to the way he had appeared on that first day in school. He looked bigger somehow, and behind his eyes something was missing.

'Did you know she is really good at drawing? Maybe you could draw us?' Percy said, turning to his sister.

'I, erm, I already have...' Nell hesitated, wondering if this was too much, too soon. She quickly leafed through her book, trying to find a memory-picture of the boys, but in all of her drawings of the boys their faces were obscured, blank. She found a sketch she had done on the *Mab*. It was a picture of Percy and Connor, in the Dearmad, happy. 'Here, here you are... Percy,' she said as she pointed with a shaky hand, 'and you, Connor, you are sat by the fire...'

'That's good! When did you do that?' asked Percy with an expression of innocent bewilderment.

'I did it before I came into the cave,' she stammered. Percy smiled at her, still missing that twinkle of recognition or understanding that Nell longed to see. Still missing that *thing* that confirmed he was really and truly coming back to her.

The knotted, curled walls of the cave and the shadows of its crevices in her drawing all mirrored the reality. This picture had been a premonition. She saw it now.

She put the book down. 'I hadn't been here before, when I drew this.'

'That's clever, that you knew what'd be like. I don't think I'm any good at drawing.' Percy smiled haplessly.

'You would be if you tried. You're always too busy doing other stuff, it's the same at home,' said Nell. 'I like drawing things that I've imagined, or rather, things I have seen in my mind. I'm good at picturing what places will look like and what will happen in the future. It's a skill I have. Although I'm having trouble seeing what will happen at the moment, in this cave.'

'And us? Did you *imagine* us?' Connor was becoming more and more agitated.

'No. No, I didn't.' She hesitated. 'I know you both. I've known Percy since I was born, before even.' Nell was speaking more forcefully, she was unable to control herself any longer. All the locked-in emotions of the past four days were rising, ready to explode. 'Percy is my twin brother and I've come to take him back home, and if you know what's good for you, you'll come too.'

Connor looked angry, shocked. 'Percy, it's time to go fishing.'

Percy stood up. Without saying anything more, he walked slowly towards Connor. His movements were precise, almost mechanical. Silently, the two boys dived into the pool.

The cave was quiet, and eerie.

'YOU WON'T WIN!' screeched Nell.

She slumped on to her bunk, her head in her hands, a tear of exhaustion rolling down her cheek.

Softly, a single piece of paper glided down from the very top of the cave, and dropped delicately by her side like an autumn leaf. She reached for it. Before even opening it up she knew who it was from.

It's time to come back.

Nell let out a loud, pained, orchestral scream that comprised nearly every sound that a human could possibly make – sounds of fear, relief, frustration, anger. But no joy. There was a palpable absence of anything even resembling joy.

As soon as Nell closed her mouth and opened her eyes, she heard a rushing noise coming from the pool. It was a royal whirl of wind and water, but the air remained disquietingly calm.

The rocks all around her groaned and the cave made a low rumbling noise like a tired old brute waking from his deepest dream-filled slumber. The low moan of the cave morphed into a grinding creak, like a door swinging on rusty hinges.

Walking slowly, tiptoeing gently so as not to disrupt the fragile balance of life in the Dearmad again, she peered into the pool. Her sea-lions. She was sure it was them. They had followed her and were looking after her. She didn't know what it meant, what they were doing, but she saw that it was beautiful, truly beautiful, and it made her think of Marnie, it brought back home. Home was with her. She closed her eyes and pictured the pinnipeds whisking her back to Mam, wherever she might be. And she knew what she had to do.

Chapter 36

The Hardest Face to Draw

NELL

Nell opened up her book to a blank space that stared back at her. She tried to keep her mind clear but the sounds of the cave were distracting her from the calm that the sea-lions had brought with them. Her friends were long gone now, and the sounds of the cave felt riotous. Frustration welled up inside her, and a red fog descended. Screaming as loudly as she could, she instructed the cave to '*SHUUUUUT UUUUUP!*'

The sounds of the cave, those groans and creaks, began to fade. She focused her mind on her own echo and the gentle

238

ring in her ears left behind by too much noise. The noise of the cave. The noise of her own thoughts.

Silence returned to the Dearmad and it felt, suddenly, like the lights had been switched off, black-out blinds drawn. All that was illuminated was a vision of her mother. It was not a drawing, but a soft moving image playing out in front of her eyes. It felt real and delicate. Nell did not see Dina as she was, in that world that existed beyond the end of the jetty. She was not the Mam who tested Nell on her spellings and times tables in front of the fire, or even the Mam who said goodbye to them at the door with Otto and Marnie standing by. It was Mam as she was that very day. She was sitting in a wicker sun chair with a huge round back to it and a stool for her feet. There were cushions upon cushions around her, the sun on her face, but blankets covered her.

Nell got closer. She squinted her eyes to see clearly. Her mam's face was the same but it was now covered in deep wrinkles, like an old woman's. Her eyes still sparkled, but they were tired. This was not a vision of the future. This was *now*. Goldie walked around in the background. He was pacing. Did he know that they were all at sea? Did Mam know? Is that why she looked so old? Had the worry done

239

this to her? Nell felt responsible. How could she have let all of this happen? Although she couldn't hear a sound from the picture in front of her, Nell watched her mother's thin, tired lips say the words, 'rest easy, they are safe'.

Nell leant in further, she could almost touch Dina now. She leant in and she saw something. A dark shadow. She leant further but was scared that the picture would burst like a bubble; pop like a delicately blown ball of glass, only to shatter into a million sharp pieces. What was it? She inched a little, then a little more. Silence returned to the cave. Dina and Goldie, the chair, the cushions, the deep wrinkles, they were all gone. But she had seen enough.

Nell held her pencil and the picture drew itself. Mam's eyes with their sparkle, her hands with bulbous veins, her cheeks with their wrinkle, but her smile still with its glow. It was Mam full of life, sitting within the grip of death.

In the corner of the picture, there it was. That dark shadow she had needed to lean in to see. It was there and it was as clear as day, now. A bird.

Chapter 37

Cave 1: Connor 0

NELL

'It's rained!' shouted Connor, pulling himself from the pool and running straight to the bucket. He threw a suspicious glare at Nell. 'I'll get this fire nice and big again, *she* has let it go out.'

Percy walked over to Nell's bunk – she had been asleep, recovering. 'You missed a good swim!'

'I can't breathe under the water and my scuba gear is still down the tunnel. I don't think I'd even get to the bottom of the pool or out of the cave without my ballast.' She complained.

Percy looked at her, confused.

'Why don't you go and get it then, instead of being all grumpy about it?' shouted Connor across the cave.

'You could come with me? I'm scared I wouldn't get back up on my own,' Nell lied. She didn't want to leave the cave; she felt sure Connor would find a way of blocking the chute behind her.

'No. I think we'll stay here, thanks very much,' Connor grunted.

Percy looked at Nell blankly.

'Listen, Percy. I need to show you something. Something in my book.'

'All right.' He smiled.

Nell opened the book. She lay it on Percy's knee as he sat next to her, and she left it there. He stared at the page, a blank smile still pasted on his face, the smile of someone with no past to regret and no future to worry about. Nell waited. Watching for his face to change, for the robot smile to finally shatter. She didn't want to hurt him. But if her plan worked, it was going to cause him pain. It would be the pain he needed.

First there were two blinks. Then he raised his hand to his chin, rested it there. He went to gasp, but nothing came out.

He twitched in his seat, itching to move; his knee started to jig up and down in his old familiar way. His body shivered and Nell saw goose bumps all over his arms. His hand slipped from his chin and rested on his neck, stroking his gills, as if he had forgotten they were there.

His head swung quickly towards Nell. No longer smiling. 'Why do you have a picture of my mother?'

Nell's heart leapt into her throat; she was stunned but knew instantly that she had to keep her cool.

This was enough.

This *might be* enough.

Just enough to get him to leave with her.

He didn't *need* to remember that she was his sister and twin. Remembering Mam was enough. She resisted the crushing urge to ask him what he remembered. She wiped away a tear and breathed deeply, trying not to let any more tears escape; the feeling burned in her chest. She let the picture speak to him.

'Can you take me to her? She looks...'

'I can. I can take you to her,' whispered Nell. 'Do you remember why you are here? This isn't your destination, this was only supposed to be a stop-off for you, but the Dearmad, this cave, it's... it's keeping you here. It has some kind of power over you and Connor.'

Connor was no longer busy with the fire. He was staring at Nell and Percy, untrusting, with a look of anger on his face.

'Connor, this cave is cursed, it's changing you. I think—'

'We don't really care what you think,' snarled Connor.

'You need to hear this, Connor. Percy still remembers home, don't you Percy?'

Percy didn't make a sound.

Connor slowly edged closer, fury in his eyes. But all Nell felt when she looked up at him from her bunk was sadness, not fear. Maybe if they'd been friends, maybe if she hadn't been so jealous of him, she would know how to reignite his memory.

'How can I do it... how can I bring you back?' whispered Nell beneath her breath.

'What? What are you saying?' Connor commanded.

Nell took a breath; she steadied herself, not sure how to explain. 'Janie... can you remember Janie, your mum? And Jonah, he's your dad and he works on the *Monabeg*. Remember, you used to live in Limiona... and you came to Kipneash...' Nell was desperate, but she couldn't get to his heart. 'I'm sorry,

Connor,' said Nell as she shook her head and wiped away a tear. 'I'm sorry. I don't know what to say to help you remember.'

Connor stared at Nell; she thought she saw a flash of softness, but it wasn't so. He was even more angry than before. 'If you want to leave, then *leave*,' he snarled.

'We were never friends, not really. I never gave you a chance. I was jealous, I've always been jealous of gillies. It's no wonder you don't like me right now, you never really have. But there's no reason to hate me. All I want to do is *save* you.'

Without changing his expression, and in what seemed like an unconscious move, Connor lifted his hand to his neck and stroked his left gill.

'That's it!' Nell exclaimed.

'What?' asked Percy, confused.

'Your left gill, Connor, you always do that... you always stroke it... it's like a tic... do you know why you stroke your left gill?'

Connor frowned. His left gill was clearer than Nell had ever seen it before, but without all of the scabbing she noticed how tiny it was, barely even there.

'You have a weakness in your left gill. It's caused you trouble all your life. Don't you remember? You were so ill, but you got well for a while and then swimming with Percy helped make you even stronger. The weakness is still there though, in your gill... You aren't like Percy... The Dearmad has taken a greater hold on you, Connor, because you aren't strong enough to fight it. The curse isn't just making you forget, it's changing you. This anger you feel, it's not me, it's the Dearmad.' The words were spouting from her mouth in a desperate frenzy that she couldn't control. Connor's expression, however, had not changed.

Nell looked at Percy as he stared blankly, once more, in her direction. *What if I lose him...? I must be quick...* she thought.

'Connor, you never stood a fair chance against this place. Now, you must either let me help you, or you must let Percy and me go without you.'

Connor didn't flinch. Nell's words made no impact. The old Connor had gone; she'd let him slip away when she was thinking only of Percy. His skin now had a ruddy pallor and his back seemed straighter, giving him a few more centimetres of height. His eyebrows were furrowed, lowering towards his hard, angry mouth, lips slightly pursed. The curse had found Connor's Achilles heel, his weak point, and had preyed on him. The Dearmad had turned him into the person Nell saw standing in front of her now.

In a final attempt to bring Connor back, to restore just enough of his memory to save him, Nell began to draw, furiously scratching at the page with her pencil, willing an image of Janie to take shape. 'Come on, come on...' she whispered.

Connor stood over her, staring at her book. He leant down and grabbed it from her, then picked up her diving pack and hurled them both to the edge of the pool. The bag and the book fell to the floor. 'I think it's time you left, don't you?'

'We've all got to leave, Connor,' said Percy.

Nell let out a breath of relief.

'What? Why would we leave?' spat Connor, his fury beginning to show in his tapping foot and angry stare.

'Doona...' mumbled Percy.

'You remember Doona?' said Nell, shocked. Her shivers began to fade, she felt strong.

'I know that's where we were going, there's something there that can help my mam.'

'Yes! *Our* mam,' Nell said.

'I can't go home now. No one must stop me from going to Doona. You mustn't try to stop me. I don't know why, there is something, I don't know, I'm confused... I... you wanted to stop me... you tried to stop me before, I think,' stammered Percy.

'There is a boat outside this cave, and there are people on that boat who want to help you get to Doona and then back home. Percy – and you too, Connor – *you* can lead us there: me, Otto and Marnie. *You* know the way. We'll follow you, make sure you're safe – you believe me, don't you?'

In the stillness, Connor stood watching. 'I'm not leaving here, but *you* are!' he yelled as he leant down again and grabbed Nell by the arm. Confused, Nell didn't fight back. She could have overpowered the old Connor, back home in Kipneash, but not now. Now Connor was filled with such fury, she was not sure what would happen. His eyes showed no softness, the cave's curse was like venom strengthening his bones. With his grip on her arm tightening, Nell stumbled and tripped as Connor dragged her across the cave to the pool.

'Who *are* you? I think you should go. You want to go. I know you want to go. But *we* don't. *We* will be staying right here,' growled Connor.

'Connor, this isn't you, you aren't like this! It's the curse – you aren't strong enough to fight it, it's taking you over. Why do you think all this stuff is here – the bucket, the beds, that awful blanket? People have lived here before. But where are they now, Connor? Where are they now?'

'You need to go, and you need to take your stupid book with you,' Connor said as he pushed her further towards the edge of the pool.

Nell followed the line of Connor's eyes and saw that his gaze was fixed on the spot on the floor where her book lay.

'You and your stupid pictures... always scribbling... trying to confuse us... well, it won't work on me,' he said in a venomous whisper.

In a scramble and a rush, both Connor and Nell swooped to the floor and grabbed at the book, trying with all their might to pull it from each other's grip. With one ferocious tug, Nell finally snatched the book from Connor's hands, and quickly stowed it in her diving bag as Connor watched, raging with anger.

'Take your precious *stuff* and go!' he shouted, seizing the bag just as Nell closed its zip.

With a single, mighty, indignant swoosh of his arm, Connor hurled the bag into the pool. Nell gasped as she watched her bag, with her precious book inside it, fall down into the water.

'This is madness, Connor! I'm not going without Percy.' She found it hard to see through the tears that were rushing down her cheeks and stinging her sea-sore skin.

Connor dropped his chin to his chest, closed his eyes and breathed deeply, like an athlete catching his breath. His arms hung down, but then they slowly began to tense. He made tight fists and he began to raise his arms like he was lifting heavy invisible weights. His eyes and mouth opened wide; his pupils were huge, a deathly black. Out of his mouth came a high, loud screech that made the walls of the cave quiver. Just as Nell's cries had unlocked a low rumbling groan and a grinding creak in the walls of the cave, now Connor's voice was doing the same. Nell felt instinctively that the sea-lions would not come – it would be something else this time.

Nell was close to the edge of the pool. She looked down behind her and saw that, from deep within it, a cloud was rising, swirling and churning. It was white and it shone in the midday sun, which was flooding into the cave. Nell looked closely – the beautiful mix of colour was like paint escaping from a brush as it is swilled in clear water. Purple and pink circles made shapes like the roses from Mam's garden. Roses that had not been seen since the summer; the bushes had grown wild and furious as Mam's tiredness kept her from all of the places she loved.

But this cloud was not beautiful and peaceful. As Connor's scream stopped, so did the cloud. It stood still in the water and showed itself for what it really was. Not one united cloud, but a bunching of much smaller shapes which were beginning to emerge as tiny objects moving independently of each other. Nell looked even closer, drawn to the mesmeric shapes.

Nell was crouched down now, at the edge of the pool. Connor came up behind her. Percy walked slowly, steadily and with great calm towards his friend and his sister as they stared into the water.

Connor's arm slowly outstretched towards Nell.

'She can't breathe under water, you know. She's not like us,' Nell heard Percy say in a slow whisper. 'Don't be scared, Nell. They're like jellyfish. They won't hurt you, so long as you stay calm – but that means you can't swim in there. Don't move your legs.'

And then Percy's whispering calm stopped.

'Let them take you!' he screamed.

Percy was giving her instructions for how to not die. In this terrible moment, balancing on the precipice, Nell put her trust in her brother.

As she broke from the trance, Nell was only aware of what was happening for the smallest of moments before she hit the water. Connor had pushed her in.

The thin, spindled spaghetti legs of the strange creatures of the pool were wrapping around Nell's limbs. Too frightened to even open her eyes, too scared to twitch, she heeded Percy's warning. She did not move. She let the jellyfish have their way, taking her where they needed to. But she knew that if they kept her here, under the water, for longer than a minute, she would be lost. A minute and a half and she would be gone forever. She counted. Ten seconds. Eleven seconds. She missed the calm of her diving mask, she missed hearing her heart beating, hearing each breath going in and going out. She could hear movement, bubbles rushing and heavy swooshes of water around her.

And then, a heavy weight.

Thirty, thirty-one. Eyes tight shut, sore from the salty water.

Another heavy push, and then something else, a hand?

Thirty-seven, thirty-eight.

She calmed her thoughts and opened her eyes, still too scared to move.

It was Percy, wild-eyed and right in front of her. Pulling her down, down, down. He smiled and pointed up. Nell's eyes followed the line of Percy's finger. The cloud was passing, dissipating, they'd forgotten she was there, she'd stayed so still, unmoving. Being calm had saved her life – for now.

Suddenly, Percy let go of her and darted down, out of sight. She wanted to protest, she wanted to scream, '*never let me go!*'

Fifty-eight. Fifty-nine...

Chapter 38

The Patient

NELL

'I think she's coming round,' Nell heard a voice say. It took her a moment to realise the voice was talking about her, and that it was Marnie's.

Marnie pressed on Nell's chest and listened to her breath. With a guttural cough, water spewed from Nell's mouth on to the deck of the *Mab*. Marnie, Otto and Percy gasped in relief.

Percy coughed. His eyes were losing their focus and his feet were unsteady.

'Whoa, whoa boy! Sit down!' Otto guided Percy to the bench and put a blanket around him.

'Where is Connor?' said Marnie.

'I couldn't, I tried... but...' Nell whimpered. 'I need to go back.' She began to insist, but her body didn't follow her plea. Her legs were weak.

'What to do?' muttered Marnie to herself as she shook her head.

Otto wrung his cap in his hands. 'We needs to sail. This boy is in the thrall of that cave, still.' He sat next to Percy and wrapped his arm around the shaking boy. 'The clocks are static. That cave has still got him. The wind is calling us away, old girl. We needs to get this boy his strength back, that's no question.'

'You're right. We need to get Percy to Doona, and fast.' Marnie stared at the Dearmad.

'Connor doesn't want to leave, Marnie. But things are getting worse for him in there. He's angry, there's a fury...' Nell shivered.

'The cave will break him eventually. We shall return, and we shall hope for the best.'

'What if we're too late?' Nell whispered, afraid of the words she was saying.

'Doona is not far now. We will return.' Marnie was pretending to be sure in her decision – Nell recognised it. 'But now, you both need to rest. I have a tin of chicken soup. It's not like the real stuff, but it'll do. With crackers – no bread, I'm afraid.'

The talk of food seemed to make Percy's eyes open more widely. He stood up, blinked five or six times, his eyeballs rolled until all you could see were the whites, and then they shut as he collapsed.

Otto caught him. 'I'll take him for a lie down, poor lad. He's exhausted and confused, I should imagine.' Otto scooped Percy up and led him below deck.

'Connor doesn't remember a thing, Marnie. He's... he's not himself any more.'

'He is still Connor. He is just in a great deal of trouble,' said Marnie, stroking Nell's back. 'You're shaking, my dear. You need to get warm and let your body rest.'

'I'm OK. I'm not cold. I was scared, in there.'

'Did Connor fight you, dear? Did he hurt you?'

'I'm not scared of *Connor*. It's the Dearmad. It *listens*, and it *responds*. It makes these strange noises... Do you believe me?'

'I believe you.'

'I was scared, but I would go back, to save him. He has a few matches left, but not enough to keep him going for long. It gets so cold at night, Marnie. I need to go back,' said Nell, decisively. She lifted the blanket off her body and tried to get up.

'No! You stop right there. We will return, I promise, but not now.'

'It has to be me. The Dearmad didn't steal my memory. I survived once and I will survive it again.' Nell looked pleadingly into her grandmother's eyes. 'I couldn't save Connor when I was scared of losing Percy. But now there would be nothing to stop me. I can save Connor. I know I can.'

'Please, Nell, you must sleep. It would be a fool's errand to try and recover him now. Neither you, nor Otto, nor myself are strong enough to retrieve him by force when he is so filled with rage. We must wait until he is ready.'

'You seem so sure.'

'I wish I was, Nell. But for now, this is what we must do,' Marnie sighed. 'All we can ever do is what we think is right.'

Nell caught sight of her diving bag.

'What is it, darling?' asked Marnie.

'Percy let go of me, in the water. But he didn't leave me. He went down, to find my pack. Percy saved me and he saved my book.' Nell smiled. Marnie covered her again in the soft blanket. The warm sun that shone down on the *Mab* did the rest, bringing warmth back to Nell's cold and weary bones.

Otto emerged on deck, shaking his head, which was capless once more. 'The boy's exhausted.' He sighed. 'We needs to get clear of that cave, it's still working its worst on him and we's got to go before it takes more.'

'Doona is close. Fynlo is close,' Marnie whispered.

Chapter 39

Not a Moment Too Soon

NELL

'He's awake! And he's talking! The lad's awake!' Shouts came from the cabin. Nell dropped her book on the deck of the *Mab*, losing her footing in her rush. Picking herself up off the floor, she ran down the stairs.

Otto had barely left Percy's side in the two days that they had been sailing since leaving the Dearmad. Marnie had taken over captaining the *Mab*; she had adopted a new conviction in her navigation, aided by her birds, and no one questioned it. Otto had kept Percy hydrated by tipping a tiny spoonful of water into his mouth every time the boy began to stir. But Percy had only shown the vaguest signs of life.

When Nell clattered down the stairs, Percy was sitting up in bed, colour in his cheeks and a smile on his face. 'Hello, do I know you?'

'Otto, I'm your old pal Otto.'

'I'm sorry, Otto. I just feel a bit strange. Like I needed a really long sleep.' He yawned and stretched as if he was waking up from a nap by the fire. 'But now, I need to get out of this bed.' Nell, Marnie and Otto looked on, stunned. Too stunned to try and stop him, they watched as he lifted the sheets off himself like they weighed a ton.

'*Cuidado, chico!* Slow down! Where are you going?' asked Marnie.

'I'm going for a swim, obviously,' said Percy. 'I have to.'

Nell moved out of her brother's way as he dragged himself up the stairs to the deck, one step at a time.

A chorus of caution came from everyone's lips, warning him to stop, but he did not listen. Before any of them could think of one wise word to stop him, he jumped into the clear blue sea. It was only the shadow of rocks far, far below reminded Nell that it was the ocean and not the sky she was peering into.

'He hasn't been able to walk for two days, and now he's diving,' Marnie said, calmly. 'I knew we were close.'

Otto grabbed his binoculars and surveyed the horizon with a frown. With a blank expression, the kind that comes with shock, he handed his binoculars to Nell. Before raising them to her eyes, she had already seen it.

'We're there,' Nell said, her eyes fixing on the distance, and then on the floor. 'I'm going to lose him again.' They watched the shadow of Percy darting away, just beneath the surface of the water. 'Look at him. It's no coincidence. We reach Doona and all of a sudden he's better. He'll never leave.'

'He remembers Dina.' Marnie draped a reassuring arm across Nell's back. 'If he won't return for us, he will return for *her*.'

'I hope so.'

Nell made her way across the *Mab* to sit on the edge in her swimsuit, ready to follow her brother. 'Just give him a couple more minutes on his own,' Otto said. He came up beside her and ruffled her salty matted hair.

Eventually, Percy's head appeared out of the water. 'Manatees!' he shouted excitedly.

Nell could hold back no longer. She jumped up, grabbed her snorkel and readied herself to dive into the water.

The *Mab* stopped dead with a sudden jolt. Nell, Marnie and Otto were hurled to the floor. There had been a thud, and then the ominous sound of cracking wood; the boat was grinding into something.

'What was that?' asked Nell, rubbing the elbow that she had scraped in the fall.

Neither Otto nor Marnie had realised quite how close they were to the uneven rocks and sand below. They were still fifty metres or more from the shore, but the water was surprisingly shallow, and the keel had hit something hard.

Marnie looked around, pulling herself back up to her feet. 'It's nothing, Nell, you go ahead – go on!'

'Are you OK?' asked Nell, rising to her feet.

Marnie nodded and smiled.

If Nell had turned back rather than diving into the sea and racing to find her brother, she would have seen the truth. She would have seen the look on Otto's face. She would have heard him murmur, 'There will be the devil to pay if the *Mab* is not salvageable, the devil indeed.'

Chapter 40

The Manatees and Someone Else

PERCY

The manatees seemed to smile as they rolled in the shallow water, prodding at Percy for attention.

Their doe eyes were positioned so sweetly, downturned on the sides of their fleshy heads, that they instantly demanded affection. Huge and humble. Big and gentle. They glided slowly in the crystal waters, flippers flopping towards the white sand.

With his arms folded and his feet crossed, Percy smiled his big, wide smile and pretended that he was ignoring them.

They gently prodded him for attention. Beyond the manatees, Percy could see Nell's legs, anchored firmly in the sand as she dipped her head under the surface, a spectator to his fun. He recognised a feeling of guilt and remembered that Nell was not gilly. *Poor Nell*, thought Percy. Thoughts were seeping into his porous mind, filling him back up with memories. The memories weren't specific, but they conjured up feelings that were recognisable none the less.

As Percy rolled in the water, submerged in the world of the sea cows, he suddenly noticed more legs appearing in the water. These were dark brown, muscly and hairy but much too long to be Otto's. Percy and Nell both lifted their heads from the water.

Slowly Percy raised his eyes. He felt a silent recognition that he couldn't place. Percy watched his sister like he was looking for road markings. Should he know this face? Was it known to her? Nell's eyes were wide, as if she knew who this man was. But she didn't say a word. In a stunned silence, Nell was taking the man in with her eyes, just as Percy was.

'Hello, *principessa*. We haven't met, which is unforgivable on my part, but I am truly honoured to address that now, my dear,' he said with a regal tone. He extended his hand to Nell, who shook it politely.

'You've got Mam's eyes,' whispered Nell. 'Are you Fynlo?'

'I am.'

Percy felt like he might recognise the name... *Fynlo*. And Nell was right, he did look like Mam.

The strange old man with the long hairy legs bent down to Percy next. His eyes were a striking, bright sea-blue, almost translucent, with flecks of deep dark-blue. They were magnificent. His teeth gleamed in the sun. He had a little grey stubble on his chin but his hair was the blackest of black. His eyes smiled at them. He was a friend, not a foe. The wrinkles confirmed it. They were happy wrinkles made by smiles, not frowns.

'Hello, my boy.' The man extended his hand again, this time to Percy. 'Fynlo Shearwater. Your grandfather.' he beamed. 'You also have your mother's eyes, dear boy. I was wondering when you would get here. I had an instinct that you were coming, so I've been on the look-out for days. I must say, you took your time!' Fynlo pointed to the sky where an albatross circled then flew away. Fynlo placed his hand under Percy's arms and lifted him up so that he could inspect the boy's gills at eye level. 'Hmmm, you've been in the wars, have you not?' He was tall and strong. He dropped Percy back down into the sea. 'Where's your mother?'

Percy searched for something to say, but words eluded him. The picture was hazy, only beginning to come into view.

'Ah.' Fynlo sighed. 'That's why you're here, isn't it?'

Percy turned to Nell, not sure what to say. She simply nodded.

As Marnie slowly approached, wading through the clear azure waters, Fynlo rushed to her and took her bags. 'What a sight for sore eyes you are,' he heard Fynlo mutter as Marnie simply whimpered, 'Oh, how I've missed you.' Percy looked away as they embraced and he felt a flash of kinship with Nell as they both rolled their eyes.

'So, you've met the twins?' said Marnie, eventually.

'They're twins? I have missed a lot, haven't I!'

'Percy and Nell. Percy is a gilly like you, Fynlo. Nell is—' Marnie stopped herself short. 'I was about to say Nell is not a gilly. But I'm not sure that is really the right thing to say. Nell is... well, she is something else.' And she gave Nell a wink. 'We have a lot to catch up on. But not now. *Más tarde*.'

Fynlo smiled and nodded.

''Tis the greatest pleasure to meet you, sir,' said Otto, reaching out his hand as he waded through the water towards them, the last one to leave the *Mab*. 'Otto, sir, the name's Otto.'

'Pleased to meet you, Otto,' replied Fynlo. 'And Dina, is she here too?' A look of concern flooded Fynlo's face.

'She's with Goldie. They went south,' said Marnie as she shook her head solemnly. 'She's... surviving. But I think you must have gathered now that she's the reason we're here. Fynlo, she's suffering. Our girl is in a very bad way.'

'Come to the island with me. We have a broth cooking, we can talk.'

Brought together by their love for Dina, the bravery of Percy, and the determination of Nell, the crew of the *Mab* made their way on to Doona, while the manatees rolled in the perfect waters.

Chapter 41

A Plan Has to be Hatched

NELL

'Are there many people here, Fynlo... I mean... Grandad?' asked Percy as they walked into camp. Percy had a new bounce in his step. He looked different, Nell thought.

Fynlo stopped walking and turned to Nell and Percy. 'You can call me Fynlo, or you can call me Grandad. In fact, you could call me Derek or Sue or Apple Crumble for that matter! It makes no difference to me... it's just so good to have you here!' Fynlo looked at them both, and Nell immediately felt the warmth of Mam in the glow of his smile.

'I'd like to call you Fynlo,' Nell said, smiling.

'So be it!' Fynlo said, patting her on the head. 'Well, this part of the island is where we vacation. By the sea. We have gazebos and tents, but you'll come into the clearing with me later and you'll see – we have established quite a sophisticated set-up on the island. It was nothing, really, when I arrived. A few settlers living in tents. But we've made something really wonderful. And, best bit is, we all live in tree-houses. Would you believe it! There are, what... twenty-six of us now. Yes, that's right. Excluding *you* dear people. All oldies like me, Marnie and...'

'Otto,' said Otto, quietly.

'Otto, that's right, forgive me,' said Fynlo raising his hat in Otto's direction and extending his hand to him once more as they walked. 'Yes, this is a place where people just on the brink of leaving it too late come to enjoy old age in good health. We don't get many young people here – too much to leave behind, no reason to take the risk.' Nell noticed Fynlo look at Marnie when he said this.

'When's the last time you had someone new here?' Nell asked.

'Oh, years! We had two new folks about six years ago. This place has a knack for making visitors want to become residents. But I suspect that won't be the case for you. I suspect your visit is planned to be fleeting. Is that right?'

'Yes, that's right,' murmured Marnie as they followed Fynlo deeper into the island.

When they got to the camp, they sat in a circle on rickety stools, around a small fire required only for cooking. The sun was warm but not oppressive, and there was a gentle breeze that swaddled them as they sat.

'Fynlo, we're here—' began Marnie.

'For the tree? Yes, I thought as much. But you can stay a night, or two?'

'One. We'll stay one night,' said Marnie. 'You see, it's nearly Christmas.'

'Ah, so it is!' said Fynlo. 'I forgot all about Christmas – funny isn't it?'

'How could you forget Christmas?' Percy whispered to Nell, dumbfounded by Fynlo's revelation.

Nell smiled. The island was accelerating her brother's return.

'Dina has been away in the Indian Ocean, and she expects us to be home at Christmas... I am sure that she will be there, waiting.' Nell felt Marnie's hesitation and it bothered her. 'It would break her darling heart if the children weren't home for their birthday. And, well, there's another issue...' Marnie's voice trailed off. The next bit was almost too difficult to say out loud.

'You see, Fynlo, we had somethin' of a stowaway who's... ah... there's no easy way... There's a lad we lost along the way, he's stuck in the Dearmad,' Otto explained.

Fynlo's eyes widened and his face tensed, contorting into something resembling a frown. He rubbed his ear and then his mouth. The happy giant, benevolent and colourful in every feature, suddenly looked like an angry headmaster. 'That cave. That *cave!*' he snarled. Composing himself, Fynlo stood up. 'No doubt you've had word from your birds – you have one watching, surely?'

Marnie nodded. 'I had some news yesterday, it's not looking good.'

Nell stared at her grandmother. Marnie hadn't shared this nugget of information. 'Marnie, why didn't you say? You can't suddenly start treating me like a child, after everything that's happened,' she barked. Marnie looked, all of a sudden, so tired and weak.

'But *chica*, you *are* a child. I wanted to give you a rest from worry. You haven't drawn a thing since the Dearmad, and you should take that as a sign that your mind is tired – it needs space from these worries.'

Everyone fell into silence while Nell searched for a retort, but uncharacteristically failed to find something to say.

'Otto, and my dear, dear Marnie, you both must be exhausted,' said Fynlo in his deep, reassuring drawl. 'Sleep. Rest. I shall take these young people to explore Doona.' He said 'Doona' in a low purr; it was a noise coming from deep within him, it wasn't just another word. 'I can see that time really is against us.'

'I's gotta check on the vessel, seems we coulda did some damage on our approach just now,' began Otto, breaking off to yawn.

Before Nell and Percy had even finished a cup of water and a sweet honey biscuit, their grandmother was fast-away in her deck-chair. Surprisingly, so was Otto, the urgency of checking on the *Mab* overtaken by the urgency for sleep. Fynlo placed a soft blanket over Marnie and brushed the hair out of her face as she drifted into a deep slumber.

Both Otto and Marnie had their feet anchored on dry land, and the worries of the sea slowly hid themselves away, at least for now.

Chapter 42

A Lesson in Strength and Where We Get it From

PERCY

'Can we stay in the sea a little longer, Fynlo?' asked Percy, as he and his grandfather made their return to Nell, who was basking in the shallow waters. Soft coral coves surrounded the island and Fynlo had already showed Percy and Nell exactly where to go to find the most beautiful coral and multi-coloured anemones that any person would ever see.

'No, no lad. It's time to see what you came for. It is a miracle of the land, not the sea.'

They walked deep into the island. Percy pictured the first settlers here, chopping back the trees and vines with knives; now there were rugged paths, which Fynlo seemed to know like the back of his huge, hairy hands.

Nell and Percy walked behind him in silence, but all around them was noise. As they got further away from the gentle churn of the sea and the slow cooling winds of the shore, the breeze sounded different. There was a whistle through the trees, a rustle in the leaves. The symphonic sound of harmonious song birds and trouble-making monkeys felt unfamiliar and magnificent.

Something shot quickly past Percy's ear, making a loud screeching noise.

'Whoa, what was that?' said Nell, looking at her brother. 'Was that a lemur?'

'She's right, lad. There are indeed monkeys, but they tend to laze about at this time of the day, over on the south of the island. Now these,' said Fynlo, pointing to the trees but not needing to look up, 'these lemurs like to show off.'

'I thought lemurs were from Madagascar? Unless somehow we have ended up in Madagascar – it feels just as far from home...' whispered Nell.

'You aren't in Madagascar. And really, you aren't so very far from home,' Fynlo said, cryptically. 'It just takes some grit and determination to get here, but the rewards are bountiful! This island is the most magnificent place on earth, I truly believe it is!'

Fynlo fell silent. His pace slowed for a moment before he stopped and looked back over his shoulder at Percy. The constant smile that rested so effortlessly on Fynlo's features was all of a sudden replaced by a sadness that didn't seem to fit with the happy crevices and laughter lines around his eyes.

'It really is quite wonderful, but that's not to say it's perfect. There's a lot I miss about home. That's why I would never ask you to stay. Life here wouldn't be right for you.'

'I understand that, Fynlo,' said Nell, pushing a branch out of her way as she walked behind Percy. 'Kipneash may not have the coral, or the manatees, or the rest... but it has a lot going for it too, don't you reckon Percy?'

Percy felt a memory rumbling in his head, churning like thick cream that would soon become butter and oil the rusty cogs of his mind. He carried on walking, silently.

'We like school, don't we, Percy?' Nell was beginning to sound desperate so Percy nodded. He carried on walking. The memories were there, waiting, but some were proving slow to return.

'School is important, Nell. It's good that you enjoy it. I bet you're rather studious, aren't you?' smiled Fynlo with a hint of pride in his voice.

Nell blushed.

This feels familiar, thought Percy. Even though his sister pretended to be immune to embarrassment, her cheeks would always betray her. She wasn't good at taking compliments. The same was true of Goldie. Percy was beginning to remember these things.

'Home is so much more than that, though, wouldn't you agree?' Fynlo continued. 'Home is where you learn to be a human. You learn to work hard, strive, behave decently. It's where you learn how to choose who to listen to, who is worth a damn, and who should be respectfully ignored. Home is everything. This is no place for children who are still learning how to be... how to be...' Fynlo grappled for the right words; his fingers and fist twisted and fidgeted as if he was squeezing a piece of fruit to test if it was ripe.

'Good?' offered Nell.

'Yes! That's it! It's so simple. Home is where you learn the most important thing of all... to be good, kind people who are ready for the world. It sounds so simple, but it is *everything*.'

Nell was quiet for a moment. 'I know what you mean.'

'Well, I don't,' said Percy as he carried on walking, using a cane of bamboo to whack the bushes that got in the way of his path.

'Yes you do, Percy,' argued Nell, with a sudden, unexpected urgency. 'You *do* know. It's like when Goldie tries to make us cook dinner. He says there's no greater kindness than in feeding people well. He says everyone needs to know how to make a nutritious and hearty spaghetti bolognaise.'

'Nutritious and hearty? That's a bit high-and-mighty, Nell,' interrupted Percy, with a grin. 'It's just pasta and sauce.' He remembered how much fun it was to tease Nell when she so obviously wanted to be taken seriously.

'It certainly is not *just pasta and sauce* if you make it the way Goldie does,' huffed Nell, her brows fixed in a frown. 'And that's not the point anyway, Percy. Goldie says it'll change your life for the better if you can offer someone a dinner full of goodness and made with love. He says—'

'He says a lot.' Percy winked.

'Now, come on, you two,' said Fynlo with a chuckle. 'She's right though, Percy, these things do matter.'

Pictures were slowly forming in Percy's mind. He smiled to himself, remembering the time he wore sunglasses to chop onions with Goldie, so that his eyes wouldn't sting. Percy was getting used to the feeling of memories floating back into his brain; it felt like the fluff of a dandelion seed floating on the breeze.

'Goldie always says we have to be kind before being right,' said Nell, prodding Percy with her own stick of bamboo.

'That's exactly the stuff I mean. He's a man of good sense, your father.' Fynlo released a long sigh from his lungs. 'I wish you could stay here forever, but this is no place for people who are still learning about the world. Home isn't just where the heart is, it's where the heart is built.'

'You look a bit like Mam.'

Fynlo and Nell stopped, briefly, and looked at Percy. Something in Fynlo's musings had teased back a fully-formed memory for Percy to feast on. Percy saw his sister attempt to hide a grin.

'There's a reason I look like Dina. She's my girl. And that's what you are doing here. You are here to *save* your mother. And that's what we must try to do.'

Chapter 43

What We Came For, and So Much More

NELL

Eventually, the children and their grandfather made it to a clearing in the middle of the island. They had trekked for at least two hours and Fynlo had introduced them to a whole gamut of wild fruits and nuts that they feasted on throughout the journey

Nell watched Fynlo as he stood in the clearing with his eyes closed, raising his smiling face to the sun. He was not a savage, although he sometimes looked it, with his wild eyes and his penchant for foraging, eating with so much enthusiasm that more food seemed to settle on his face and down his front than actually in his mouth. He had a well-to-do accent and he had a gentleness about him, especially with Percy, whose memory was still so clearly fractured, split into shards that he was slowly pulling back together.

Doona had accelerated her brother's recovery, but Nell knew there were still pieces missing, important pieces. She had to remind herself to be forgiving, and that Percy's often confused or blank expression was evidence of how damaged he still was. *Be patient*, Fynlo had whispered to her and patted her reassuringly on the shoulder, but she couldn't help but huff with frustration when Percy offered no new response to her tales of home. She bit her tongue and told herself that it was less than twenty-four hours ago that Percy was lying in bed, on board the *Mab*, unable to walk.

Nell wanted to get to know Fynlo, but soon they would be on their way. She closed her eyes to test whether she would be able to picture his face when it was not in view; she tried to burn his image into her brain. A day was not enough time to get to know Fynlo properly, and tomorrow they would be gone. Nell caught hold of his big, hairy hand and held it tight. *You don't always remember the thoughts you think inside your head, but you always remember the things you do.* She comforted herself with the thought of her book; she'd draw him, she'd see all this again.

The clearing was exquisite; it was more open than the rest of the island and the sun shone brightly and beautifully. The sky was spotless, save for the occasional purple, pink or bright orange bird that would swoop down low to take a look at the strange new visitors. There was a pool that was fed by two crystalline freshwater streams.

In the middle of the clearing was a tree. Many of the trees on the island had the look of palm trees – like stretched-out pineapples, or wispy tall trees with thin trunks and long branches. But this tree could have come from Goldie's garden. It was old. It had gnarly knots and roots and the remnants of ancient veins seemed to wrap around its unfeasibly thick trunk. So thick that even if Nell, Percy and Fynlo had joined hands, their ring of arms would not nearly make it all the way around the trunk. Their fingertips would not even touch.

Around the tree were six saplings – tiny trees in comparison, no higher than Nell's shoulder. Their small branches reminded Nell of Connor's spindly frame when he started school, and a knot formed in her stomach at the thought.

She noticed a black hole that looked like a fire pit in the place of a seventh sapling; the kind of black mess left behind on the beach when Goldie and Dina let them toast marshmallows there in summer. The hole was creviced and ugly and it felt dangerous. No grass grew near it and no insects loitered around it. *Mortha Dhagg*, she thought.

By some unspoken agreement, Nell and Percy felt the need to bow to the magnificent tree. Neither had shown reverence to a tree before, but they both instinctively knew that it was necessary here.

'Thank you for keeping us safe on our journey to you,' whispered Percy.

'Please keep us safe on the journey back home,' said Nell, glancing at Percy as she spoke.

A tremendous, shocking gust of cold wind whooshed its way through the clearing, and as the leaves of the tree did a shimmering dance, five hundred birds or more rose from its branches. They sang a mesmeric song that was not quite in perfect tune, but was bewitching nevertheless. The trees, the birds and the rattle of the wind made a cacophony of wonder which sent shivers down the spines of the three onlookers. The hair stood up on Nell's arms and legs, her jaw shook and her teeth chattered, despite the warmth of the sun.

'I do not ever ask for anything, not really.' Fynlo was wringing his hands and looking to the top of the tree. 'Sometimes I've had to call upon my grit, my will and my wiles, that's true. But I have never been left wanting. You have provided, faultlessly. But this... this thing I have to fix now... this problem with Dina... it has me stumped, and I am here to ask for something more.' Fynlo scratched his head, he looked embarrassed to be asking for help. He cleared his throat and carried on. 'My child is flailing. She is monstrously sick. The woman I raised from a sapling. And I know... I know I left her, and not a day passes when I don't struggle with that regret. But I am asking you *now*. These children, they are good young people and they understand responsibility. They will understand this responsibility. This *grave* responsibility. They will know the rules. They know what is right. The boy, Percy, he will be a Gatekeeper one day. And Nell...' Fynlo turned to look at his grandchild. He was silent.

Nell felt the absence of words. She was used to the painful absence of words; the absence of words about her absence of gills. Percy was the special one. Percy was the gilly. Nell was used to silence when it came to her.

Fynlo cleared his throat. He had more to say.

'Nell has gifts from the sea and the sky, combined in their own mysterious way. It is not *dangerous*, not like we always feared it could be. Nell sees time in the winds of the sea. She is beginning to see the truth in a way that no one else can.' Fynlo looked at Nell; she felt her eyes filling with tears. 'One day soon, as she learns to command her gift, I believe Nell will be able to see the truth in people, in their past and in their future. I believe that she will know who to trust, and who not to trust. Your sapling will be safe under her care.'

A sudden force of wind stopped Fynlo in his tracks and knocked the children to the floor. The sound of the leaves brushing up against each other and the wind punctuated Nell and Percy's groans as they pulled themselves back up to their feet. The birds sang a pained song. They were now making a disquieting, tormenting plea. It was a sound that was so loud, so shrill, that the children covered their ears.

'It is time!' roared their grandfather, who raised his arms to the sky and threw back his head. With that single movement, one of the saplings began to creak and shake, and, one by one, like long spindled fingers, each of the sapling's roots liberated themselves from the ground. Through the noise of the wind and the birds and Fynlo's roars and the leaves of the magnificent tree, Nell could hear the snap-snap-snap of the sapling freeing itself from the ground. Nell thought she heard a muted faraway scream with each snap.

The sapling rose into the air and hovered there, before moving slowly towards Nell. In a single breath the wind stopped, the noise subsided and the sapling fell to the floor. Nell, Percy and Fynlo closed their eyes and silently thanked the tree.

Nell hadn't noticed the razorbill had been following them, tracking their journey. It swooped down and, in a single motion, plucked a leaf from the sapling with its beak and flew away.

'Wait!' called Nell. But the bird had already gone. 'Is that OK? Fynlo, did the bird just steal—'

'It's OK. It's OK,' Fynlo reassured her.

Slowly, the Shearwaters bowed once more, before turning to each other, not quite believing what had just happened.

'Percy!' said Nell 'Your eyes! They're blue!'

'They've always been blue,' replied Percy, confused.

'No, they're *really* blue! Like, *that* blue!' said Nell, pointing to the sky. She stared at her brother. 'And your *gills*! What the... Your gills! They're *golden*! They're not red any more. They're shining!'

Percy had a look of frozen shock on his face. He raised his fingers to his neck and stroked his gills. 'They feel soft, and a bit scaly. They don't feel delicate any more, oh no... am I... Fynlo...am I turning into a fish?'

'Ha!' barked Fynlo. 'No, boy! I remember that happening to me. I am far too old for it now, but once upon a time I had golden gills too. You'll see the difference. You'll *feel* it.' Fynlo laughed heartily and wiped away a tear.

Nell looked down at the sapling which lay delicately at her feet. She felt like she was under a spell, not wanting to look away in case it should somehow disappear. Her gaze was only broken when Fynlo scooped up the sapling and placed it gently in some muslin cloth that he had pulled from his knapsack. He handed the bundle to her.

Nell faced the tree. She bowed her head, not knowing what else to do. 'Thank you,' she offered, gripping the sapling carefully in her arms.

Nell wondered how she would explain what had happened to Marnie. She looked up and saw a dark shadow-like bird making its way gracefully across the sky. She wondered whether Marnie might already know.

Chapter 44

A Big Decision

PERCY

That night, the travellers gathered themselves around a gently burning stove in the centre of Doona's village. The children dipped their feet in the freshwater stream that trickled through the centre of the village. Otto marvelled at the irrigation system and the bounty of vegetables that grew in the camp.

The village was organised with pinpoint precision, each area designated for a different purpose. It was a horologist's dream – little cogs revolving seamlessly for the good of the big machine. The residents' homes were simple, solid tree-houses and huts built with whittled sticks and wood, each with a brightly coloured curtain door. There were a few animals living in the village, but they were pets, not livestock. There was a sweet smell in the air, and that was down to the perfect mix of dried flowers and herbs that were hung daily, like incense, above the main fire. The settlement even had a library.

The island was home to a community of people whose age it was impossible to work out. They appeared old, but they were spritely, they swam with Olympian vigour and their skin shone. Their eyes were bright and their teeth were whiter than white.

'Everyone is so shiny, Percy, maybe they're ghosts,' Nell joked, wriggling her fingers at him and making 'oooooh' noises. He grimaced with a muscle-memory reflex; Nell had always made fun of him being frightened of anything remotely ghoulish. He remembered how annoying it was.

'That's not funny,' he grunted.

They ate root vegetables with fish wrapped in vines and roasted on the fire. The adults drank Fynlo's mead, made from the island's honey. Nell couldn't identify the delicious, sweet vegetables, and when she asked Fynlo to repeat what they were called he just laughed at her. 'What is anything called? Call them what you will my dear, you'll not find these in your supermarkets back at home. Name them what you like!'

It had been a long day and the children were battling sleep as Otto, Marnie and Fynlo shared stories about the sea. Nothing could compare to what Fynlo saw every day on Doona, but he was kind and listened with his bright eyes as Otto talked about the cold waters he called home.

Percy learned about *Mortha Dhagg*. It felt like new information, but he didn't trust his memory not to be playing tricks on him.

'I didn't know about this before, did I?' he whispered to Nell. She shook her head, eyes as wide as he had ever seen.

And as Otto talked about the cold waters of home, and told familiar tales that Nell had clearly heard a-plenty on the *Mab*, Percy felt pride in belonging to this crew. They were family, and not just in blood. Otto too. He wanted to know Otto better, like Nell did. He saw their bond and wanted in.

Nell, Otto, Marnie and now Percy – they had become a pack of wolves. A collective of adventurers. He was part of this tribe. There was only one thing missing.

Connor.

* * *

Otto gently nudged Percy awake.

'Wake now, boy. Us old timers have bored you to sleep with our tale-telling. Let's get you pair off to Sleepsville.'

Otto guided the twins to their home for the night with a caring arm that conjured the feel of Goldie's protective embrace. The slightest thing could trigger a memory in Percy's slowly healing mind; he let this one settle and he basked in it for a moment.

As they climbed the ladder into Fynlo's hut, the three travellers stopped still and surveyed the walls in stunned silence. They were adorned with memories. Pictures of Dina as a child, pictures of Kipneash, black-and-white and techni-colour memories. And Marnie. The walls were peppered with pictures of Marnie too. Where there had not been enough photos in his haul from another life, Fynlo had filled the gaps with ink, paint, charcoal.

Otto shifted uncomfortably and wrung his cap in his hands as he cast his eyes around the room. 'Good night, kids,' he mumbled as he helped them into the hammock beds. Silently, Otto backed out of the hut and climbed down the ladder.

'This is pretty weird,' whispered Nell.

'I like it,' Percy whispered back. 'It makes me think of home.'

'I'm not surprised, it's like a shrine or something,' muttered Nell. 'Did you see Otto's face?'

'Yes.'

'He looked worried. Are you thinking what I'm thinking?'

'I don't know, Nelly. What *are* you thinking?' said Percy, impatiently.

'Hmm.' Nell smiled. 'You haven't called me *that* in a while. So, is your memory totally back now? Did the tree bring it all back?'

'I think so. I suppose I'll be the last to know.'

'I guess. But if you want a second opinion, I think I've got my annoying brother back.'

'Thanks.' He grinned, with an eye roll for good measure.

'I'm worried that Marnie might not come back with us,' Nell said with a frown.

'What?' Percy craned his neck so that he could look his sister in the eye. 'She's got to.'

'Yes. She's got to.'

They were silent.

'What's it like, for you... being *here*?' whispered Nell.

291

'Nelly, I'm tired... aren't you?' replied Percy.

'Please Percy, I need to know. Is it going to be hard for you to leave?'

Percy searched his thoughts for the right words to say. He could have brushed the question away, or concocted a lie to pacify Nell. But he sensed that she would see through him if he answered with anything other than the truth.

'Everything feels easy,' he said, eventually. 'Like you probably feel all the time, I guess. I feel like I've always been trudging uphill through mud, but now I'm running on Kipneash bowling green, you know? It's just clear and bouncy and *easy*.'

'You'd get banned from the park for doing that.' Nell smiled.

'I know.' Percy chuckled.

'Is it really *that* hard for you though, at home?'

'I never thought so before. But, yes, I think it is. I never knew any different. I thought the tiredness was normal.'

'The naps after swims?'

'Exactly. I spent more time asleep than awake some days. And I thought it was normal to be itching to swim, literally itching in my skin when I needed the water. Even the feel of my gills – I just accepted it as the way it had to be. But I'm a strong gilly; it makes my stomach knot when I think about how Connor must've felt, when he was at his most ill. He's never been strong. It must've been... I don't know. Like torture.'

The hut filled with heaviness and regret.

'But now you know how it feels here...' whispered Nell.

'Yes. Now I know what it feels like here, what 'normal' feels like, I know that going back will be hard. And I'll want to come back here.'

He heard his sister sniff. He could imagine her holding back a tear, he'd seen her do it enough times. She didn't argue with him; what could she say?

'I've got too much to miss, Nell. Mam, Goldie, you, home,' said Percy. 'Here isn't perfect. Now shut up Nelly, I'm trying to sleep.'

Chapter 45

The Wreckage

NELL

'It's no good. It's no bloody good. Agh. It's just... *no good.*'

Nell rubbed her eyes as she peered out of the hut into the bright light of the morning. Otto was pacing the floor. She could hear him cursing and fussing.

She gathered herself up and climbed down the ladder to meet the morning.

'What's the matter, Otto?' she said, yawning.

Deep in thought, Otto gave a little jump and made a small squeal. He looked sheepish. Almost ashamed.

'We got a problem.' His hat was nowhere to be seen, and his face was bright red. His eyes looked wet and there were big patches of sweat under his arms and down his back. Nell could see that he had been working on something because his fingers were covered in fresh scratches and he had dried oil marks on his face and forearms.

'What's the matter?' asked Nell.

'It's the *Mab*.'

Percy appeared from the hut looking confused.

The children followed Otto as he led them to the shore where Marnie and Fynlo were stood, knee-deep in the water, staring out towards the open sea. It took Nell a few moments to understand what they were looking at: not far in the distance, floating in the crystal sea, were plastic pots, flasks, life-jackets, bags. The contents of the *Mab*. The remains of a sail floated in the distance and a bird sat, perched delicately, in the middle of it, as the fabric poked its creases above the sea, a floating fabric island in the distance.

'We hit silt when we arrived yesterday, but it must have been rock too. I comes out yesterday and patches what I can. But I musta missed...' Otto hung his head. 'Never, never

295

should this've happened. Good for nothing. Never has I had a calamity like this... I blames myself.'

'The *Mab* was almost completely under the water when we got here this morning, darlings,' Marnie explained, looking to the distance where the boat should have been. 'And now, this is all that's left.' She nodded towards the bobbing remnants littering the sea. 'Flotsam. I'm sorry. *Je regrette...*' Percy and Nell showed their terror on their faces. The *Mab* was their only way home.

'I didn't want to worry you all. I should have seen it was a lost cause yesterday, not a patch-up job. We was all so tired, my handiwork was wanting,' Otto said, shaking his head. 'I's ashamed, I is. This fault is *mine*.' Otto looked down into the water, hands on his hips, too embarrassed to look up. Nell took his hand.

'Are you OK, Fynlo?' Percy asked, noticing his grandfather fidgeting and huffing.

'Ah, all right...' He had a look of submission printed on his sun-stained brow. 'Look, there is a solution, possibly. But...' He hesitated. 'My boat. I mean... I built a boat. Mine got destroyed, much like yours has.'

'I thought you swam here, like me?' asked Percy.

296

'No, I came prepared for the long haul.' Fynlo blushed, locking eyes with Marnie. 'I salvaged what I could and crafted a new boat from the old. It's quite a boat, actually,' he said with pride.

Otto grunted. Nell looked at his face, scrunched into a scowl.

Fynlo's cheeks flushed again. 'You might be wondering why I didn't mention this sooner...'

'Go on,' coaxed Otto, his voice carrying an unfamiliar force.

'Well, yes, that was a poor show on my part. The thing is, it's my lifeline, to get back home. The selfish part of my heart didn't want to let that go.'

'I understand that. But these kids gotta get home.'

'You're right, Otto. And of course you can have it. Of course you can.'

'This is your home, darling,' Marnie said to Fynlo as she reached out for his hand. 'I understand why you came here. Goodness knows I tried more than once, but it was always out of my reach. I am no swimmer. I'm not even a sailor, not really. It took my birds, Nell's instincts, Otto's seafaring and Percy's determination.'

'And *the pull*,' Percy added.

'Yes. I would never have got here without you all. And, if you will allow me, I will make this my home now.'

Fynlo gripped Marnie's hand in his and bowed his head. Nell saw his knuckles whiten, like he was clinging on for life.

Percy and Nell looked at each other, and then at Otto, who stared at his feet.

'But... but... we *need* you!' exclaimed Nell.

'Please don't fear, Nell, you don't need me.'

'Yes, we do! We can't do this without you! What about Connor? What about your birds, surely we need *them*?' Nell roared. She had predicted this, but the reality of it stung like the waves on her sea-sore battle scabs. Marnie's words were a bolt to her chest.

'You *can* do this without me.' Marnie smiled. 'And I think you know you can. With Otto. With Percy. And with my birds. You can get home, *and* you can get Connor back. I believe in you.'

'We gotta leave now, girl,' Otto said to Nell with a calming hand on her shoulder. 'There's no more time for floundering about. We gotta get Connor, we gotta get to the boy.'

'Nell, I think you know that even if I am not with you on that boat, we shall be together in the sky, and in your book.

You know that, don't you? We shall be together always. And this is not the end.'

'Do you *really* have to stay?' asked Percy.

'My boy,' said Marnie, taking hold of Percy's hands as she looked into his blue eyes. 'My boy. I am *supposed* to be here, with your grandfather. I will forever be grateful to you for leading us here. Your sister will retrieve Connor, I know she is capable of this. But you cannot go back in there. Promise me you won't go back in that cave.'

Percy nodded, not sure if he was lying. Not sure if he could let Nell do it alone. 'I promise.'

Marnie turned to her friend. 'Otto. I love you dearly,' she said with a softness that sounded like song, like velvet. Percy and Nell tried to respectfully conceal their embarrassment but even in the gravity of goodbyes they could not help but give each other a look of disgust as their cheeks turned pink. 'I will always treasure our friendship. You have been my most faithful and adored companion for all these years and I will miss you every day...'

'Say no more, old girl. Say no more. You can trust me to deliver this precious cargo safely home. You can count on it,' said Otto bravely.

'There's one last thing, then,' said Marnie, with a smile on her face. She raised her arms up to the sky, and she tilted her face up to the sun. The others looked up to see what it was that Marnie was looking at with such wide, sparkling eyes. The long flow of her clothes waved in a sudden breeze and, seemingly from nowhere, the sky was filled with starlings. They were making patterns and swirls over the vast, shimmering blue sea. Marnie clapped excitedly, then placed her hands on her heart. 'I knew we would see them again. They'll be with you, my loves, *ma corazon*! They'll bring me news and they'll keep you safe. The tides may be against you, I will send word of what I know. *Se fuerte*! Be strong!'

Chapter 46

The *Marnie*

PERCY

Fynlo's boat was a jumble of the island's strongest wood intertwined with wreckage bounty, salvaged and threaded together by Fynlo's talented hands. It was truly beautiful. And colourful too. He had dyed the wood and polished it in myriad colours; the boat was a veritable rainbow of the tides. Everyone stared as Fynlo removed a mesh of hand-woven vines that had been spread over it with care.

'The *Marnie*!' announced Fynlo, gesturing towards the small calligraphy inscription stained on to the side of the boat.

Marnie made a small noise, something like a hiccup mixed with a sigh. She put her hand to her mouth, surprised, and smiled.

'How's he managed to keep his boat gleaming like that without all the potions and chemicals from the boat yard, eh?' Otto shook his head and whispered to Percy, who was similarly impressed. 'My crusty old mitts are callused to kingdom come with my years of boat polishin'. *Oxide*-this and *sulphates*-that, I tell ya.'

They pulled the boat, upon its trolley, to the shore and into the water, deeper and deeper, until the trolley was no longer needed. Otto was the first to climb aboard. 'This will be a joy to captain, yes it will. It took us a little more than two weeks, give or take some, to get us 'ere. I say' – Otto licked his finger and held it up to the sky – 'another two-an'-a-half weeks and we'll be sat warm by your fire. If we get a shufty on, we could make it for the New Year.'

'No! No, no, no!' shouted Percy in horror 'No way! Christmas. She said she'd be home for Christmas. We *have* to be there when she gets back.'

'Percy—' Nell tried to calm her brother, but he was in no mood for listening and cut her short.

'Mam's coming back for Christmas, so we have to be there,' he repeated.

'We'd better get going, then!' said Otto.

While the others salvaged what cargo they could from the *Mab*, Fynlo took Percy aside and ushered him away to the freshwater spring.

'Percy. Are you ready to say goodbye to this place for good?'

Percy took a moment to think. 'No. I'm not. I can't tell Nell, but I'll be back here one day and when I return, it will be forever.'

'I thought as much,' said Fynlo with sad eyes. 'Plant that sapling. Keep it safe and don't let your friend, what's he called...?'

'Connor.'

'Yes, don't let Connor know about it, but he'll need something after he's been in the Dearmad so long. Give him a leaf, a twig at most, but say it was all you could reasonably take from here – a leaf for Dina and a leaf for him. That's all he needs to know. It's just a white lie. The sapling cannot be risked. There is a strength of will that is needed to cope with the power of that tree,' Percy listened intently as his grandfather spoke. 'You proved that you have that strength when you left the Dearmad.'

303

'It was Nell who saved me.'

'Yes, that's true. But she could only save you because something inside you clung on to your past, to the good.' Fynlo shook his head solemnly. 'The truth is, boy, that sapling is a great, great gift. But it is also an enormous responsibility. Bad things could happen if it got into the wrong hands. Ask your mam about *Mortha Dhagg* and the seventh sapling.'

Percy nodded.

'With your sapling, you will be kept from ever needing to come back here. It is a true gift, I can't tell you how many times I begged for a sapling myself, so that I might return to Kipneash. But the island never conceded. You are *incredibly* lucky – you do know that, don't you? If looked after, that tree will allow you to live in balance for the rest of your life, in the world that you know best, with those you love best.'

'But it'll never be like this. Not like Doona,' said Percy.

'This place is like heaven on earth, but when you are away from everything you know... well, a person's mind can make a hell from a heaven, it is true.' Fynlo bent down to Percy, gripped him tightly by the shoulders. 'Now you've been here, life is not ever going to be the same for you, my boy,' he growled in a low, guttural whisper. 'That sapling is your piece of Doona, guard it with your life.'

Percy nodded seriously. He understood. He would indeed guard the sapling with his life.

Slowly and carefully, Fynlo pulled something from his pocket. It was small but perfectly spherical and glossy, almost glowing, maroon-brown. 'If ever you are in danger, this nut will help you. It's the purest fruit from Doona. But don't eat it a moment too soon, the effects will be short lived. Just long enough to get you back here. All right?'

Percy placed the nut deep in his pocket and tapped it twice, to make sure it was safe.

'Right,' declared Fynlo. 'Let's collect some fresh water. Your shipmates are going to need that. Strange isn't it? They're going to need all this water even though they'll see nothing but water for the foreseeable, and they think *we're* the anomaly!'

And as Fynlo laughed a big hearty laugh, Percy looked up at his grandfather's magnificent gills, remembering his mother.

All that mattered now was getting home. Getting them *all* home. And that included Connor.

Chapter 47

Goodbyes

NELL

Nervous excitement sent shivers of energy rushing through Nell's limbs like electric spikes. She tried to stop her teeth from chattering. She was not cold, neither was she scared. But they were off again, and this time she knew what was coming.

As they said their goodbyes, Marnie and Fynlo tried to make light of it all, with smiles and well-meaning advice. *Keep drinking water, you must avoid dehydration. Give our love to everyone at home. We are never very far away,* they said, as if they lived on the mainland or in the city rather than a world away. It was comforting for Nell to hear it, though, even if it wasn't true.

With one final look back at the heavenly white shores of Doona, with the manatees circling the shallows and the bright green glow of the lush hills in the distance, Nell wondered how they had done it. Three humans and one gilly had made it to Doona. She clutched her book to her chest and looked to the starlings overhead.

They had salvaged a few tins and had enough of Fynlo's biscuits, grains, pickled vegetables and dried fruits from the island to keep them going for two weeks. They would need fish to supplement their diet but Percy would take care of that. They were set. They had water and had managed to rescue their purification apparatus from the *Mab*, even if it did look like it had fought a battle of its own, the cracks mended with tape and held together with wire.

They were off.

Nell refused to believe this would be the last time she saw Marnie. They locked eyes as Fynlo and Otto pushed the *Marnie* out to sea.

'Big things are going to happen, little one,' whispered Marnie.

'I will miss you, Marnie,' said Nell as she caught the whisper on the breeze.

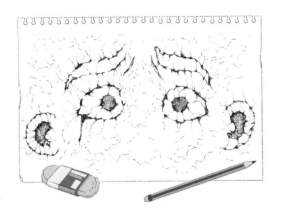

Chapter 48

Sea and Sky, Sky and Sea

PERCY

'You coming?' grunted Percy.

'You know I can't go in with just my snorkel,' Nell hissed.

Two days had passed and there was no sign of the Dearmad, their next stop. Connor's future depended on it. The mood on board the *Marnie* was heavy.

'Yes you can, but *whatever*,' said Percy dismissively. He turned his back and jumped in. He would be in the water all day, only returning to set them back on course if they faltered, or if there was something spectacular to share with Otto.

The monotony of the trip back was only made worse by the urgency of it. It had only taken them two days to get to Doona from the Dearmad. It was taking longer this time, and every hour felt like a lifetime. Percy spied as Nell confided her thoughts, fears and questions about the future to the razorbill, and it seemed to understand. It had a look of knowing as it tilted its head to listen. With Nell so locked up in her own fear, Percy had no one to confide in. He had worries too.

'When I close my eyes, I can see the walls. They're all gnarled. I can see the pool. I can hear the groans and the drip, drip, drip of the tin bucket,' Percy listened to her explain to Otto as they looked out to sea, the boat lit only by torches and the swinging lamp. A shot of twisted fire rose in his throat and he closed his eyes, breathed out. Marnie was right, he could never go back to the cave.

Nell was quiet and her patience was short. There was nothing Percy or Otto could say or do to make things better.

A heavy burden rested on them all: it was Nell who had to save Connor, and Nell alone.

On the morning of their third day at sea, Percy woke to the sound of Nell scribbling fiercely in her book. He stood over her and watched as she started to shade in a whole page

310

with tiny, dark graphite circles, squares, lines, angular shapes that he didn't recognise. He made her cocoa and brought her a honey biscuit. After an hour, she stopped and stood back from her book. Percy looked. He could see that what she had drawn was a wall – the stony, gnarled wall of the Dearmad cave, with two dark, pained eyes looking out from it.

Chapter 49

Old Friend

NELL

And then, it was there.

It was there in front of them, looming as it had before.

It was time to go back into the Dearmad.

Percy and Otto stood in silent acceptance of the uncomfortable truth: they were sending Nell back in.

'If it weren't for the boy, poor Connor, I'd be away from that cave, *flank speed*,' said Otto, not taking his eyes off the horizon as the Dearmad got closer, gentle wave by gentle nudging wave. 'Ah, there's no use.' He threw his hat on the floor. 'I can't do it. I cannot let you go again. I'd be happier running the gauntlet my own self, I would.' Otto shook his head as he flung open a trunk to retrieve his wet suit.

'It's OK, Otto. It's OK.' Nell picked up Otto's hat and gave it back to him, steadying him. 'What would we do without you to sail us home? We can't risk that,' Nell reassured him. She rested her small, soft hand on his scarred and weather-worn arm. 'I know what I'm doing. I've done it before. I can do it again.'

This was the most certain Nell had felt in days. Her mind was clear and she knew what she had to do.

'I hate waiting, that's been the hard part,' said Nell with eyes fixed on the Dearmad.

'Really? We hadn't noticed.' Percy smiled. He had never been very good at sarcasm; his big benevolent grin took away the bite. 'Seriously though, Nelly, you do know I'd go if I could, don't you?'

'I know.' Nell nodded. 'And, you know, you mustn't follow me in there, even if you feel like you should. If I'm gone too long... don't follow me. We can't risk it. I'm not worried any more. I know I can bring Connor back. I don't know how, yet. But I know I can.'

They drifted closer to the cave in silence. Percy placed a leaf in Nell's hand.

'What the...? I thought... The sapling's safe, isn't it?' Nell felt the leaf between her fingers, it felt fragile, like it could blow away on the wind, melt away between her fingers. She held it in front of her and felt protective. How could Percy have just pruned a leaf away? Each piece of the sapling was sacred. Did he not understand that?

'It's safe. Fynlo said Connor would need something, that it would be OK to give this to him,' assured Percy.

Silently, she tucked the leaf into the waistband of her swimsuit and lowered herself into the water. No wet suit, no scuba gear. The cave still had all of that. No bag. She was not planning on staying.

'You've got 'til sundown this time. Not a minute longer. We'll be after you if the sun sets and you ain't back. You hear?' assured Otto.

'I understand,' Nell said as she slid into the water.

Swimming into the canyon was not an option without her scuba gear. She would need to take the same route in through the false cave again, through the rocky tunnel. There would be no escaping through the pool this time, either.

Nell pushed away the fears and doubts that were beginning to circle in her brain. She concentrated on the feel of the water, the strength in her legs, her breathing and her stroke. She found a hypnotic rhythm, and with it her senses felt sharp, she felt *strong*.

In, ouuuut... in, ouuuut....

She would keep her brain focused and ready, she was ready, she was ready.

In, ouuuut... in, ouuuut... She stopped thinking of the person Connor had become, the Connor she had last seen. She thought only of him at school, at their house, with his mother. She thought of Janie.

In, ouuuut...

In, ouuuut...

Her breath quickened but it kept the same rhythm.

In, ouuuut...

She could do this.

The approach to the cave had more of a swell than last time; it was not as inviting. The sea lurched towards the rocks in an unsteady shunt. It was pushing her towards the Dearmad as much as the cave seemed to be pushing her away. The sky was greying but the blue of the morning was peeking through the corners. This was the first sign of threatening skies since being in the Doona core ring. Something was amiss. The sea was saying it, swelling with an anger that was spilling out of the cave. Nell bruised her knees as she lifted herself into the false cave, remembering how she felt the first time she was here and how she felt now. Frightened, but fearless.

Out of the water, her skin shivered and her heart pounded, with both exertion and the anticipation of what lay ahead. *I'm here for Connor... I'm here for Connor...* she repeated in her mind, pushing away the fears and doubts once more.

Her breathing changed. It was a more urgent rhythm that pulsed through her veins and around her head.

In, in, out.

In, in, out.

Her kit was still there. She would not be able to carry her scuba gear through the tunnel, so she left it where it was, to be collected on the way out. She was glad to have it there. It would make her stronger for the swim back to the *Marnie*. She gave a nod of her head. Now was not the time for any kind of overstated celebration or feeling of achievement. She could only feel achievement if she succeeded in getting Connor back.

The tunnel. She snuck up it, just as she had the first time. It was easier this time, her muscles remembered what they had to do. Unhealed scabs tore on the rock but she did not flinch. Her battle-weary legs were stronger now. Cuts and bruises were common friends that showed how far she had come.

In, in, out.

In, in, out.

In, in, out.

She took a moment at the bottom of the last vertical climb. She listened, just as she had last time. She heard a low muttering. It was Connor. She could not rely on his help to pull her out of this final obstacle as she had with her brother.

In, in, out.

She placed her feet and hands on the walls of the tunnel either side of her. She had to push hard with her legs so as not to lose her grip and slip down. Tiny shuffle by tiny shuffle, she made her way up. Gripping until her fingers turned white and her hands ached.

She fell.

Right back down to the bottom.

So close, but so far.

Seven times, this happened. She kept count.

In, in, out.

But then, she did not fall.

Those hard and unforgiving walls of the tunnel had tried to defeat her, but not this time. Eighth time lucky.

But the moment she laid eyes on Connor Price was the moment that she really understood how lucky she was.

All of the obstacles in her way, and all of the fears she had harboured, fizzled to dust when she saw Connor. None of Nell's journey mattered now. Nothing could compare to what Connor had endured.

No more *in, in, out.*

The noise of her thoughts fell away into a vacuum. She set her eyes on Connor and all fear was gone. All anger disappeared. All plans of how to capture or convince him passed away. No trickery would be needed. There wouldn't be a fight. The Dearmad could take nothing more from him. It had sapped him dry.

She tiptoed close to him. The Dearmad no longer echoed with the music of the sea and the wind. The boys' calls and laughter were foggy memories. The cave groaned in the eye of a storm that was raging around it. Below the cacophony was the resonating sound of a gentle sob.

As she got closer to Connor, she saw that his arm was covered in tiny little rocks, like he had been swimming and the coarse stony sand of the beach had stuck to his wet skin under the glare of the sun. But this was no holiday beach trip. The sand was not clinging to his sun-silken skin; it was part of him.

'*What have you DONE?*' Nell screamed to the heights of the cave. She willed the cave to fall, to crumble, to admit defeat.

The storm outside was rolling within the bowels of the Dearmad.

Connor was slumped on a rock, leaning into the wall of the cave. His body was moulding itself into the deep crevices of the cave walls and it was turning the same colour as the grey and pinking rock.

'I... never... noticed... them,' Connor wheezed, straining to speak. 'The faces... in the walls...'

Nell looked closely at the wall next to Connor, and sure enough, she could just make out the outline of a person, a man, asleep against the rocky wall, a person of rock. It was not a trick of the light, not a satisfying pareidolia in a cloud-speckled sky.

The storm was getting worse. The cave walls shook in tiny, terrifying vibrations. Nell knelt down. It was true – Connor's arm had been turning to rock, with small slivers of shiny skin showing through like open wounds. His hand, resting on his knee, was completely transformed already.

'Oh, Connor,' she breathed, crying as she pulled him close, peeling him away from the living rock of the Dearmad. 'Will you come with me?'

Connor stared past her.

'Connor, it's time to go,' she begged. She pulled at him, but he was a dead weight. He barely shifted. 'Do you remember Port Kipneash? Do you remember Jetty Beach, and the wreckage?'

Still nothing.

'You eat all our biscuits and you sit in front of our fire. But I won't get cross about it again...' She was panicking. She didn't know what to say. Words fell out of her like water fighting fire. 'Please Connor, try to remember,' she begged.

She pressed her forehead against his and squeezed her eyes tightly shut.

Without the memory of joy there was no hope.

She pushed her thoughts out, hoping that they would land in Connor's broken soul. *Remember Janie. Remember Jonah. Remember it all.* She flooded her mind with pictures from the past: ice cream sundaes; Christmas morning; the lights of the harbour; riding her bike downhill; lying on the floor, tickled into tucks of laughter. *These are my memories, Connor, you must have some too?*

Thunder rolled in the distance and stone was falling like shattered glass from the walls of the cave. The noise was rising, gathering strength.

On the edge of giving up, as if staring down a canyon before letting go of a feather, Nell let go of her tears. They rolled down her cheeks and wetted Connor's cheeks too.

'Please, Connor... show me that the Dearmad hasn't won... You may not remember happiness, but I promise it's worth fighting for...' Nell's words came out like staccato croaks, red-raw and full of despair, barely managing to escape from the depths of her heart. 'Please Connor, will you come home?'

She closed her eyes. Amidst the groans of the cave and the roaring chaos of the storm, there was a still silence between Nell and Connor. She waited for her final question to be answered.

And then, there was hope.

Connor Price whispered one word. 'Yes.'

Nell hesitated. Fearful that she had imagined Connor's quiet response, her brows knitted together and she froze. Every muscle in Nell's body tensed. In that moment she felt like, if she wasn't careful, her whole body might just melt.

Slowly, Nell opened her eyes. She looked into the dark black holes that had replaced the shiny happy windows into Connor's soul.

It was there! She saw it, she saw that Connor was still in there. A glimmer, a twinkle; his eyes gave the smallest smile.

As if beckoned, the razorbill swooped down low, next to Nell.

And then the starlings came, and the turns and the swallows.

Birds filled the cave in a majestic rush, darting, swooping, attacking an invisible threat. Nell felt no need to cower. She had a peculiar sensation that the raging storm was her doing, that somehow she had called it here. What was it Marnie had said? *The mysteries of the sea and sky are combined in you.* She felt that somehow her grandmother was with her; Marnie had instructed the birds, and they had come. But Nell had had a hand in it too, the skies had responded to her need. Together, Marnie and Nell had called for all of the forces at their will to enter into this cave to help Nell defeat it.

The birds were rattled. They curled around the contours of the Dearmad, licking its crevices with the smooth-swoosh of their wings. Not one inch of the cave was untouched by their presence. They spun and twirled, they dashed and rushed, squawking, making their frantic cries. In the chaos and hubbub, Nell saw the albatross and she felt safe. Almost.

There was still evil at work. There was an imbalance in nature, weighing mightily on the side of the wicked force that inhabited the cave. The birds felt it, the sky felt it, Nell felt it. Together they would remedy it.

Without warning, the razorbill hopped right up to where Nell was crouched and plucked the leaf from the band of her swimsuit.

'The leaf!' exclaimed Nell, scolding herself for not thinking of it sooner. 'But what do I do with it?'

The bird held the leaf delicately in its beak and waited.

'Does he need to... what? Eat it?'

The razorbill dropped the leaf and flew away.

Nell picked up the leaf and held it carefully between her fingers. 'Open up,' she said as she brushed it gently against Connor's dry, flaking lips. 'Now chew. Chew! Come on, put your arm around my neck,' she demanded. He rubbed his back; his skin looked sore from where it had begun fusing to the rock. Nell winced at the pain her friend was in.

She helped Connor on to his feet and dragged him to the entrance of the tunnel. With each of Nell's steps, Connor's legs moved more, remembering what they were for. His joints creaked like an old man's when he did his best to walk. He would not make it through the tunnel like this. But there was another possibility...

The chute.

'This might hurt a bit, I'm not sure... ah, I don't know...' She hesitated. To jump down the chute would be like jumping from a first-floor window. The army of birds were swooping through the cave, diving at the pool, filling the deathly void with movement and sound. But the cave's own sound was competing too; it howled and yowled like a wolf maimed by a desperate black bear in defence of her young. The floor was shaking. Nell looked to her side, where the wall of the cave was nearest to her, and she saw the face of a woman, asleep, moulded into it.

'I can do it,' said Connor with a croak.

'Try to hold on to the sides with your feet and hands, if you slip... erm... push out, to the sides, hold on to whatever you can to slow down the fall. Do you understand?' Before he could answer, he was gone.

She waited a moment, took one last look at the cave. It was full of the life of the birds. It was moving and groaning. It was being defeated.

Following her own advice, she clung on to what she could while she lowered herself down the vertical chute. She fell part of the way, hands and feet now bleeding, but stopped herself on jutting rocks and fortunately placed footholds. The pain did not register, there was too much at stake. She lowered herself the last metre and saw Connor, similarly wounded but standing upright and bold at the entrance to the false cave. He was looking out. The leaf had strengthened him. The *Marnie* was less than one hundred metres away, just clear of the rocks.

Nell quickly retrieved her things and put the wet suit and scuba gear on, never taking her eyes off Connor. She felt that if he fell on the hard stone of the false cave his bones might shatter like a porcelain doll.

'The leaf, was it from D... D...' He did not know how the sentence ended.

'Doona? Yes, it was from Doona. It was from your friend, Percy.'

'Percy?'

'Yes. Your friend. He's on the boat, waiting for you. We want to take you home, Connor. To Janie, your mum.'

'Yes. I think I would like that. I think...'

The leaf had worked: Connor's body was becoming stronger by the minute, his back was straightening and his eyes were losing their empty stare. But his thoughts were confused; his words made little sense.

'You don't remember your mum, or Percy, do you?' asked Nell.

'No. But there *is* something there. Shadows... clues... I *hope* there is something still there. I think...' Connor coughed. He spluttered.

'Are you strong enough to swim?'

'Yes, I think I am.'

Suddenly, the sea took on a stillness and calm – an eerie calm. It felt unsafe. Something was happening inside the cave. Wind drew into the cave entrance like a vacuum, nearly knocking the children off their feet; it felt like a hurricane was coming.

Then everything was still again. So unnervingly still.

'What was that?' said Connor.

'I have no idea. Come on. We need to go. *Now*. Hold on tight!' Nell said before putting on her scuba mask. They held hands and jumped into the sea together. Nell was strong with her scuba gear and could have pulled Connor along easily, but he didn't need it. He was strong enough himself. Just.

Under the water, as Connor kicked for the boat and safety, Nell offered a silent thank you to the ocean. Down here, she could no longer hear the strange sounds of the Dearmad.

In, in, out.

Chapter 50

A Sea Change

PERCY

'Holy moly!' said Otto as Nell climbed up on to the *Marnie* with Connor behind her. Otto leant down over the side of the boat and with a great heave he pulled Connor aboard. Connor was shaking and Percy placed a blanket over him.

'He's safe,' Nell panted. 'But only just. That leaf helped, but he's going to need more. Check out his hand – the rock. And it's moving up his arm. We need to get out of here. The Dearmad still has him. Until Otto's watch begins to work again, we should assume we are in its hold.'

The *Marnie* rocked from side to side as Otto quickly prepared the main sail for departure.

Percy sat down next to his friend. Connor stared up at him. 'I remember now. You were my friend.'

Nell threw another blanket over Connor, then went to help Otto.

'Still nothing, girl,' Otto shouted, pointing at his watch.

Percy looked down at Connor, weak and crippled by the rock. *You were my friend. Were.* Those words bit. 'I *am* your friend, Connor. I'm Percy. I'm your *good* friend.'

'Good friends don't leave,' Connor muttered, so that only Percy could hear.

'I worked it out,' said Nell, walking back to the boys and resting on her knees. 'When you used to go swimming for fish, you always came back to the Dearmad, remember? I don't know how far you went, but it still pulled you back – we need to get clear of it now, it still has its grip on you, Connor.'

Connor's eyes were closing; he was drifting away.

'Keep him warm,' Otto called from the helm. 'Give him a blanket, make sure that shakin' don't get no worse. All that's keepin' him goin' now is adrenaline. You're right, Nell, girl, you're right. We need to get away from that cave or it'll

329

take his arm. If it makes it to his chest, his heart, it's game over. And look now.' He pointed to the cave. 'See what's happenin'?'

Otto's eyes narrowed into a stare that was fixed, unwavering, on a point in the distance. He was looking beyond Percy, Connor and Nell, in the direction of the Dearmad. Percy got to his feet and turned his gaze towards the monstrous rock too. He could see what Otto meant: the birds were flying out of the cave in droves. What at first looked like dense compacted shapes made by birds, was actually a great looming cloud of black smoke, creeping from the top of the Dearmad through the hole that had once brought the cave sunshine and filled it with life. The Dearmad was slowly disappearing before their eyes. What was once so powerful a presence, jutting angrily from the calm clear sea, was now crumbling into the sea. A huge black plume emanated from the shattering rock like the smoke from a noxious fire.

'Something evil is leaving that cave. I think I did this,' whispered Nell.

'Erm, sorry to disappoint you Nell, but you're not *that* powerful,' said Percy. 'It won't last long, there's nothing in there to burn, there's only a few—'

'It's not on fire, Percy. Something's leaving. We don't need to watch this. We should go. Connor is going to be OK now.'

Before she retreated below deck, Nell turned to Percy. 'If something is leaving the cave, where is it going to go?'

Percy shrugged. 'Do *you* know?' he asked.

'No, not for sure. But... does that cloud remind you of anything?' his sister whispered, so softly she seemed scared to speak the words that were coming from her mouth.

He shook his head.

'The black circle left by the seventh sapling. It reminds me of that.'

As Nell disappeared from view, Percy tried to ignore the chill creeping up his spine. He turned to Otto.

'What was all that? A cave can't really catch fire, can it? I mean, it's rock – fire can't beat rock.' Otto simply looked to the horizon and shook his head.

Connor was still asleep on the deck bench, so Percy decided to stay by his side, occasionally pouring sea water on his neck. When Connor had come aboard from the Dearmad, his gills looked brown and slimy, as if full of rotting algae. The leaf was working, though. They were transforming in front of Percy's eyes, slowly turning pink and shiny as Percy gently dabbed away the crusty residue for his sleeping friend.

He opened Nell's sketch-book, which had been left carelessly next to a discarded blanket.

'Paper beats rock,' he whispered, as he watched the Dearmad crumble, boulder by boulder, into the sea.

Chapter 51

The Core Ring

NELL

'What is it, my boy? What are you scared of?' Otto soothed Connor as he stirred from sleep. His skin glowed with sweat but he was shaking. The tortured look in his wild eyes told them all that his had not been a dreamless sleep.

Connor held up his hand, the rocky boulder a constant reminder of the cursed cave. He sobbed gently until sleep took him again.

'We can feed him a twig,' whispered Percy.

'Are you sure?' asked Nell. 'I gave him the leaf, when we were at the Dearmad.'

'Fynlo said we could. He said, *"a leaf, a twig at most"*. I think he needs it, Nelly.'

Nell, Otto and Percy watched as Connor chewed on a small piece of twig that Percy had peeled gently away from the sapling, being sure not to let Connor see what he was doing, and being sure not to disturb the sapling's delicate branches. Percy carefully wrapped the tree up once more, with freshly soaked bandages around its roots. It would be planted in the Shearwaters' garden and its proximity would save Dina. It was precious. Percy tucked it safely under the lid of the bench next to the starboard balustrade between two life jackets, safely out of Connor's sight.

Connor slowly took in the twig's goodness. It helped. It helped a lot. Within a few hours, Connor's gills were clearer than they had ever been before. Colour flushed his cheeks. Speckles of rock turned to freckles.

'Another leaf wouldn't hurt, would it now?' suggested Otto furtively.

'No more, Otto. Fynlo said.' Percy shook his head.

A heavy, burdensome silence had filled the *Marnie* in the days following the crew's final battle with the Dearmad cave. But things were changing. As the past returned to the boys, and as home became ever closer, they began to revel in their happiest memories once more, and joy was starting to bleed into their thoughts of the future.

While the boys swam, Nell drew, and slept. And Otto looked to the horizon. Nine days had passed, and with each one Doona slipped further from their minds.

* * *

Nell yawned as she stirred from a nap. Otto was at the helm as usual, gazing out to sea, but Nell could see concern in his usually calm expression.

'Are you OK, Otto?'

'What's that, my girl?'

'You look worried.'

'Worried? Not at all. I'm a copper-bottomed sea man, that's me. There ain't nothin' worries me out 'ere.'

There had been some favourable winds, and Percy had been a good guide. Getting home for Christmas might not be too far-fetched. But there were still the eddies to battle. It had been so easy before, with the help of the birds. Nell could see that this time would be different. Her sketches had shown her.

'You're worried about the eddies, aren't you?' Nell prodded. She approached him. 'Marnie and the birds... they got us through the eddies last time, didn't they? Marnie's birds steadied the *Mab*. Maybe they'll do it again?'

Otto nodded. 'Hmm. Maybe. We's much, much further from Doona and your gran now though. We's travelled a long way from Marnie.'

'But the razorbill... the razorbill will come,' said Nell.

'Yes, yes, maybe so. I has no doubt your gran will send her birds, but if she can command great numbers of them when we's on the edge of the core ring, on the cusp of home, so far from Doona... I ain't so sure about that. I think we needs to be prepared that we might be on our own this time, girl.' Otto took off his hat and scratched his head, and then replaced the hat as it was. 'No use in worrying. I knows what I'm doing. Your gran might be friend of the sky, but I know the sea. I ain't on me beam ends just yet!'

'I think I had something to do with the storm, in the Dearmad. Do you think that too, Otto?'

'I think there's a lot we don't know about what you is capable of, little lady.'

'I wish I knew what to do... to help us... like Marnie did.'

'Oh, that ain't your responsibility. Let me do my part – you let me guide us. I'll get us through.' Otto winked at Nell.

But Nell did feel responsible. She wanted to guarantee them safety, like Marnie had. But the sky wasn't at her command, not yet.

* * *

Nell watched the sky with the eye of a hawk. She was searching for clues, a sign of what she could do, how she could call to the mysteries within her. *How did I call that storm?... Why can't I settle this one...?* Despite Otto's words, she felt responsible.

The winds were changing. Slowly at first, but the sky was brooding, and the swells were beginning to churn the angry sea ahead. By tomorrow they could be on the other side of the eddies. They could be on the home stretch.

'Boys!' called Otto over the side of the boat. 'Boys!'

Percy was just ahead of the *Marnie* and swam back, quickly.

'You all right, Otto?'

'This is the last stretch, before we's gotta leave the Doona core ring. It's time to have one last swim in these waters. Are you doing the eddies with us, or are you going deep?'

'We'll stay together,' said Percy. 'We'll stay on the *Marnie*, right, Connor?'

'Right.' Connor nodded in agreement.

'No. Percy, Connor, you need to do this in the deep. It's safer for you. And anyway, you should be in the Doona core ring waters for as long as possible, it's what you came for, it's time for you to say goodbye to all that, to end your journey,' insisted Nell.

'But—'

'No,' Nell interrupted her brother. 'Besides, the fewer people on board the *Marnie* the better. You'll just be in the way. Right, Otto?'

'Whatever you says, Nell.' Otto nodded. 'We'll see you boys on the other side. Go deep and get through by your own selves. Me and Nell got the *Marnie*, don't we, girl?' Otto smiled at Nell.

Nell smiled back.

'Stay safe, won't you boys?' said Otto, wearing worry on his wrinkled brow as he leaned over the railing to wave goodbye to Percy and Connor.

'Don't worry about us.' Connor smiled as his head bobbed in the water next to Percy's.

'I ain't no parent, but I seen now – there ain't no rest from worry, boy!' Otto chuckled nervously. 'No sir. But, ah boy, it's a golden feelin'.'

As the boys swam away, Nell could hear Otto's low mutterings over the sound of the sea.

'What is it, Otto?'

'Tomorrow be Christmas Eve. Your birthday. I know what it means to you, to your brother, to your mam, and me old friend Marnie too. I's just asking the heavens if we might have a kind wind to push us home.'

'Can you ask for some rain too?'

'Has it finally bit the dust?' groaned Otto.

Nell nodded. The purification apparatus was all but wrecked when the *Mab* was destroyed, and now it was no longer usable at all.

'Well then we gotta get home, has we not?'

But when the rain came, and the sky finally answered Otto's pleas, they knew that they had been foolish to will the weather. The clouds smouldered above them. The force of the eddies was looming once more.

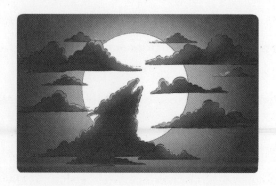

Chapter 52

Otto Battles His Friend the Sea

NELL

A black-dog cloud covered the moon, and the *Marnie* rocked from side to side like a metronome. But metronomes are predictable, and Nell knew that the sea was anything *but* predictable.

She longed for Marnie.

The boat began to rock harder, and then violently. A swell was suddenly upon them. The Doona core ring was spitting the *Marnie* out of its territory, and the force of the push was becoming stronger and stronger. The swell transformed into a strong current.

Nell stood at Otto's side as they held on to what they could, just to remain standing. A flashlight and a rope clamp tumbled from a cupboard that had lost its seal. They slid along the deck and were propelled into the sea. Nell grabbed at a tool bag as it slid along the deck next to her, preventing it from meeting the same fate.

'Go to the cabin, girl! I've got this!' Otto yelled over the now-raging storm. Water spat at them from every direction and they could only see each other when the few lantern torches on deck swayed in their favour.

'I'm not leaving you up here on your own!'

In the sway of the light, Nell caught sight of her book, lying on the deck. Quickly, she scooped it up, and rolled it, forcing the tube into the pocket of her coat. By the flailing lights of the vessel she thought she could see the starlings back in their great black cloudy formation. And there! The razorbill! The stark white of its chest was a beacon as it flew ahead of the boat. She glimpsed Otto in another sway of the light. He wore a look of determination on his face that filled her with hope. She might not be able to control the storm, but if anyone could control this boat, it was him.

As Otto barked clear orders at Nell, she followed them without question or hesitation. They were a machine. There was no room for fear. No room for rumination.

And then it happened.

A sudden lurch to starboard sent the *Marnie* crashing into the next wave with such extreme force that the boat tipped sharply to one side.

We're going to capsize... this is it... we're going to capsize, Nell thought, clinging to the port side railing with all her might. The *Marnie* was going to flip upside down, Nell felt sure. But then it didn't, it had corrected itself; or rather, Otto had used his incredible skill to pull them back to safety.

'Nell, bow to wind!' Otto called. But Nell didn't move. 'Do you hear me?' Otto yelled. 'Nell!'

Nell clung, ashen-faced, to the railing under the swaying light of the lantern. She'd just caught sight of the starboard bench.

She rushed to the railing on starboard and leant herself over the side.

'Nell! What is it?' cried Otto, single-handedly fighting to keep the boat on course. 'Nell, answer me, now! There is no time for this! Girl!'

'The sapling!' Nell wailed. 'The sapling! The starboard bench opened when we tipped! It's open, Otto and it's empty!'

Otto lurched himself towards her. He clung to the railing as he searched the deck for signs of the tree.

'Do you *know* it was in there? Was it certainly there, girl?' he shouted, pulling himself back to the boat's wheel to regain control, to keep the *Marnie* from capsizing.

She flung the sketch-book from her pocket and threw herself into the water.

'No! No! Nell! No!' Otto cried. He grabbed a torch and held on tight to the railing of the *Marnie*, shining the light out to the sea. He moved it in all directions, desperate to catch Nell in its beam.

The seconds felt like hours, time stood still while Nell searched the dark chaos of the sea. She came back up for air. In the light of the torch she saw the razorbill trying to hover over the waves, battling with the deadly wind. And then the albatross too. She knew where she must look. The birds knew where the sapling was.

'Are you there, Nell?' shrieked Otto.

She wanted to respond, but the sea gagged her. She couldn't stop her eyes from closing in the onslaught of the swell, but instinct guided her. Her limbs were being pulled in directions she could barely fathom, but she pushed back, she held control and she grabbed at the sapling.

Nell fought to make her return to the *Marnie*, gripping tightly to the tree as she swam. She saw Otto stood, precariously, on the edge of the boat. She could see him ready himself to dive, torch in hand, for all the good it would do.

'The ring!' she yelled. 'Don't jump, Otto! The ring!'

As Otto filled his lungs with air, Nell called to him once more.

'RING!'

'Nell!'

'I'm here, Otto! I'm here!' Nell exclaimed, holding on to her strength, but feeling it slip from her. 'Please hear me Otto! I'm here!' The fight was disappearing from her voice as her legs were losing their beat and the sea was pulling her down. 'I'm here!'

Otto opened his eyes. He slipped for a moment, and bent his knees low to keep from stumbling into the angry ocean.

He saw her.

A wave threw Otto back and he landed on the deck with a thump. He pulled himself up and grabbed the life ring, a fortunate remnant of the *Mab*. He hurled it to where Nell was, head bobbing above the water, then disappearing as she lost her battle to stay afloat.

In the light of the torches which swung above, Nell looked up from the depths she had been dragged to. She could see the ring floating on the surface, and she willed her legs to propel her up, to beat as hard as they might, but she sank further and began to feel the limp drag of exhaustion.

With the final grain of energy that she was able to muster from somewhere deep within her bones, Nell kicked up and grabbed the ring, being careful not to lose her grip on the sapling. Otto pulled back, and slowly Nell returned to the boat.

As Otto hauled her up from the sea, Nell clung to the sapling. She had saved her brother once more.

'Nell...'

'No... time... Otto,' she panted. 'The boat... is full... water... it's going... down.'

Nell dragged herself to her feet, adrenaline pulsing through her veins. She staggered to her bunk in the cabin as quickly as she could, stowed the sapling under the covers and forced herself back up to deck.

'Tell me what to do,' she said, regaining her breath.

Otto held her by the arm, and nodded. 'Bow to wind, you gotta release some tension in the boom topping lift,' he directed as he heaved trough after trough of water from the *Marnie*.

'Got it.' Nell winced, dodging the boom as it swung towards her.

The swells were getting worse still. The *Marnie* crashed on the waves as it hit wall after wall of freezing cold water, being flung back into the Doona core ring and spat back out again. Home had its arms open, calling them back. It was within spitting distance. So near. But then they were flung back again. So far.

The sky was spluttering rain at them in haphazard tranches. Sheets of water followed by gusts of spray, soaking them from above. Nell clung to the mast at the stern by the erratic light of the swaying torches, while Otto jetted from one side of the boat to the other, mastering the mechanics of keeping it afloat. Nell knew instinctively where to hold on so that she was not in the way of her captain, but she was tired. She was cold. Her teeth chattered and she fell to the floor and coughed so hard her body convulsed.

Every inch of the boat could be felt by the duo, every crash of every wave. The keel, rudder and skeg doing battle with the mighty force of the churning sea. The sails facing the strength of the winds. But the *Marnie* was doing well. It was doing Fynlo proud.

'Take yourself below, girl! I'll not take no as an answer this time. GO!' Otto yelled. He wasn't angry. Nell knew he wasn't angry. She followed his command.

Gradually, the waves became smaller, and the swell could not be seen by torchlight or moon, it could only be felt gently beneath the boat, no longer hurling them and confusing them. Nell curled up in her bunk, the sapling still under the covers. She would find somewhere safe for it, but for now her exhausted bones needed rest; she couldn't think of getting up.

Otto and Nell were back in home seas, cold, rocking, with grey night skies and no stars, the moon lazing sleepily behind a mask of cloud. They were safe, and the rolling wolf-clouds of death slowly retreated. Otto stumbled down the steps below deck, legs weak under the pressure of the hours just passed.

Nell was awake, but dazed.

'Girl, get these on you.' He passed her the driest clothes he could find. He wrapped her in warm blankets, combed through her hair and fed her the last of the tinned soup with what remained of the gas for the hob. '*Now* we is on our beam ends.' He chuckled. 'We are ragged and near dead. But we made it, Nelly, we made it!'

Too tired to answer, Nell allowed sleep to take hold.

'You'd've died for that tree, wouldn't ya, girl?'

But before she could answer, Nell was fast away.

Chapter 53

Doona Water

CONNOR

Deep beneath the *Marnie*, the boys swam, oblivious to Otto and Nell's reckoning with the waters that had carried them home.

Connor Price had some peace to make. Enough of his memory had been restored that he knew what he had missed. *I never saw it.* He gritted his teeth. *All this, and I never even saw it.*

Doona. Like chasing a balloon destined for the sky.

I'll forgive you, Percy Shearwater, he said to himself as he followed his friend deeper and deeper still. The water of the core ring flushed through his healing gills and there was a sweetness to it. The same sweetness he'd felt in the pool of the Dearmad cave. He hoped he'd forget that pool one day, but he feared he would never forget its beauty. There was terror in that cave, but there was wonder too.

Soon the water would be icy and hard. It would leave that familiar harsh taste in his gills, a bitter flavour; he wasn't sure whether it was the churn of the sea or the bite of pollution.

Doona must have been a marvel. He'd go there one day.

As the sea began to fight and the swells ahead became evident, Connor stayed with Percy, trusting that he would not leave him again. To lose trust now would be a submission to his scars, and it was his choice to allow himself to heal.

If only it was that easy.

Forgiveness isn't always a choice. *I want to forgive, I have to forgive.*

Connor pushed his body forward, propelled it towards Percy, who looked back at him. Connor offered Percy his good hand, as they swam together into the tail of the eddy which twisted above them.

Chapter 54

Home Waters

NELL

'It's a good job one of us is paying attention, hey Otto!' Percy laughed as Otto stirred from sleep. The air was icy but the sun was bright. They had covered their captain in blankets and sat by his side until the sun woke him. They had waited for hours, nearly the whole day. They passed Kitterlund, dropped anchor, and waited for Otto to rise.

'I can navigate, no problem!' said Nell when Otto finally came to. She was wearing Otto's cap and stood at the wheel. She had a cut on her lip and her arms were very badly bruised.

Even though smiling made her wince in pain, she couldn't help herself. The sun was shining and Kitterlund was behind them. Nell had seen a man waving from the steps to *The Sky*. But she hadn't waved back. There was a lot that she wanted to forget.

Nell let out a cough, clearing her chest in the cold winter's air. Otto started to say something, but she shook her head and widened her eyes in an effort to silence him. It worked. He simply nodded. Nell didn't want Percy to know how close they had come to losing the sapling.

'I shouldn't have let myself sleep,' Otto chastised himself, and he took back his cap and reclaimed the wheel of the *Marnie* from Nell. 'And it's your birthday! Many happy returns! No cake yet, but there'll be celebrations once we get you home, that I don't doubt!'

'Thank you Otto. It's certainly the strangest birthday we've ever had.' Percy smiled.

'You boys got through them eddies OK then?'

'Yeah, it was pretty scary, but we made it,' said Connor.

'And your hand?' asked Nell.

'It feels lighter. I think I can move my fingers, maybe just a little. But the skin is still rough. Whatever that leaf had in it must be pretty strong stuff.'

Nell and Percy caught each other's eye and immediately looked away.

Nell called the others over when she spotted a school of dolphins swimming alongside the *Marnie*. Connor and Percy didn't answer her call. They looked at each other briefly, as if they were remembering a lie they had told, a lapse in judgement, a secret not to be spoken about. Nell didn't pry this time. Being left out no longer bothered her. She had her sketch-book. She had the sky and Marnie's birds. She had grit.

And then, as the sun began to set on Christmas Eve, there it was: *home*. The moon was making an appearance once more. The razorbill was asleep on the deck and the children and Otto were huddled together for warmth. They had agreed to stay together on the deck of the *Marnie* for this final procession into Port Kipneash.

The jetty was lit up with Christmas lights, and Mam and Goldie were at the end of it, with Janie and Jonah. Wrapped up in coats and blankets, sitting on foldaway chairs. Looking out to the sea. Waiting for their people to come home. Their most treasured people. Their children.

Janie Price let out a scream and collapsed to the floor when she saw the *Marnie*. Jonah quickly sank to his knees and helped her back up, held her and soothed her with words that no one could hear over the shouts of joy from the crew of the *Marnie*. Connor was the first to clamber from the boat, a bandage wrapped around his hand. He clung to his poor mother, who shook as she held him close to her.

Nell and Percy stepped off the *Marnie*. There was so much to say, so much to explain. Not least where the real Marnie was.

Mam smiled. Her hair was jet black again and her face looked alive. Percy walked to her and he gently brushed the smooth silken hair away from her neck. Like alabaster, her gills were smooth and shone by the light, just as they should.

'We knew you would be back tonight. We could never miss your...' Dina gave a sharp intake of breath and held back her tears as she set eyes on her son's golden gills, his bright blue eyes. '... your birthday,' she whimpered.

'I had to go, Mam,' said Percy, pleading with her to understand. 'I had to.'

'I know. I know.'

'One of Marnie's birds... delivered you a leaf... didn't it?' whispered Nell, 'I saw the razorbill steal one and I hoped it would find its way to you.'

Dina nodded. 'Last night, when we arrived home.' Dina looked at Nell, her head tilted to the side a touch. She gave Nell a knowing smile. 'You're Marnie's granddaughter, that's for sure.'

Dina's shoulders relaxed and in a superhuman reflex of love, she gripped hold of her girl. Nell felt more warm and safe in her mother's arms in that moment than she had ever felt before.

Goldie locked his long arms around his three and closed his eyes.

Chapter 55

Family

OTTO

As Otto anchored the *Marnie*, the others walked back to the Shearwaters' home. He could hear their joyful sounds of relief and gratitude that Percy, Nell and Connor were safely home. There was so much for the crew of the *Marnie* to explain to Dina and Goldie, Jonah and Janie. But not tonight. The sun would soon rise on Christmas Day, and the families were reunited.

Otto gathered up the sapling. He held it close to him, careful not to let it be damaged. A leaf poked out from the blanket and it crossed his mind that to take it – for Connor – might *not* be such an awful thing to do. *Could it really do so much harm, if the boy knew about the sapling?* he wondered.

But before Otto could act on his impulse, there was a loud clatter below deck. In a flurry and flutter of wings and squawks, the razorbill appeared. It settled itself on the side of the boat, next to where Otto stood. It looked directly at him, into his eyes. Without breaking his gaze, Otto gently pulled the blanket over the sapling so that none of its leaves were exposed. And off the razorbill flew.

'What are you doing?' a young, gentle voice sang out from the shore.

'Ah, little lady, I was just packin' up your things, bringing you this before I sets homeward.'

'But Otto, home is *this* way.' She nodded away from Jetty Beach and back towards the house, where the others were heading.

'I couldn't...'

Nell let out a giggle. 'Don't be silly. This is where you'll be. I've seen it.'

And Otto believed she had.